Get the Scoop on America's Top Gymnasts!

Read all about the young women who are working hard to make the American team and fulfill their gold medal dreams at the Sydney Olympics.

- Kristen Maloney and Vanessa Atler, often rivals for the top spot on the podium—but still good friends—who are both fighting to recover from injuries.

- Elise Ray, who has been making a name for herself with big performances in major international competitions.

- Morgan White, whose determination and dedication give her an edge over her competitors.

- Plus Jennie Thompson, Alyssa Beckerman, Jeanette Antolin, Jamie Dantzscher, and updates on 1996 gold medalists Dominique Moceanu, Amy Chow, and Shannon Miller.

It's all here: in-depth profiles of the top contenders for the American Olympic team, a recap of the 1999 U.S. Championships and other major competitions leading up to the selection of the American team, and a typical day in the life of a world-class gymnast, plus much more!

Look for other sports biographies from Archway Paperbacks

AMERICAN GYMNASTS

Gold Medal Dreams

CHIP LOVITT

AN ARCHWAY PAPERBACK
Published by POCKET BOOKS

New York   London   Toronto   Sydney   Singapore

AN ARCHWAY PAPERBACK Original

An Archway Paperback published by
POCKET BOOKS, a division of Simon & Schuster Inc.
1230 Avenue of the Americas, New York, NY 10020

ISBN: 0-671-78545-1

First Archway Paperback printing August 2000

10 9 8 7 6 5 4 3 2 1

AN ARCHWAY PAPERBACK and colophon are registered trademarks of Simon & Schuster Inc.

Book design by Kris Tobiassen
Cover photo credits: background photo by PhotoDisc;
front cover by Jamie Squire/Allsport; back cover photos
by Donald Miralle/Allsport

Printed in the U.S.A.

IL 4+

QB/✖

Acknowledgments

The author would like to thank the following people and organizations who provided invaluable assistance and information throughout the writing of this book: Elise Ray for graciously and generously taking the time from her busy 1999 season to answer my questions, Courtney Caress and Connie Maloney of USA Gymnastics, Liz Shiflett of Pocket Books, Brian Schlessinger of *Sports Illustrated for Kids*, and *International Gymnast* and *USA Gymnastics* magazines.

Contents

Living Up to a Legend   1
On the World Stage   17
The Showdown in Sacramento   24
American Gymnasts Close-ups   46
   Kristen Maloney   46
   Vanessa Atler   61
   Elise Ray   80
   Morgan White   92
   Jennie Thompson   106
   Alyssa Beckerman   116
   Jeanette Antolin   124
   Jamie Dantzscher   137
A Day in the Life of a Champion Gymnast   148
Next Stop: Sydney 2000   154

Gymnastics Events and Scoring   169
Glossary   176
Gymnastics Web Sites   179

Living Up to a Legend

Sports history is full of tough acts to follow. Champions cast long shadows, and it's even harder to live up to a legend. No one could be more aware of that than the young women striving to make the United States women's gymnastics team heading to the 2000 Summer Olympics in Sydney, Australia. The Americans who make it to Sydney will not only be taking on the world's best gymnasts but will also be trying to step out of the shadow of a legendary team of champions— the Magnificent Seven.

In 1996, a proud and determined team of American women captured the gold medal in gymnastics for the first time in Olympic history. With that victory, the 1996 Olympic team—dubbed the "Magnificent Seven" by the media—not only rewrote sports history but also captured the hearts of sports fans around the world. No one who watched the 1996 Olympics would ever forget the Magnificent Seven, nor would they forget the sight of a courageous and injured Kerri Strug being carried to the podium to receive her gold medal after sealing the American team's triumph. That will always stand as one of the great moments in Olympics history.

As the 1999 gymnastics season began, the Magnificent Seven were still very much on the minds of many in the American gymnastics community. Even though the Olympics were still more than a year away, the countdown to the Summer Games had already begun. A new generation of gymnastics champions and young hopefuls—girls who had watched the Magnificent Seven's stunning achievement on TV—were about to begin their most important season ever. The U.S. National Championships were approaching and a battle was brewing for the title of U.S. champion. Beyond that, the World Championships in China loomed. As important as those events would be, they were also crucial stepping-stones on the path to the biggest prize of all, an Olympic medal in 2000.

The young hopefuls on the 1999 U.S. national team had much to look forward to. At the same time, it would be difficult for them not to look back at their predecessors' achievements with awe and admiration. No doubt, the talented teenagers on the team were facing an enormous challenge. But they also saw Sydney as a great opportunity and a chance to write their own record into the history books.

Elise Ray of Columbia, Maryland, 1998's uneven bars champion and 1999 floor exercise champion, spoke for her teammates when she said, "The Mag Seven *is* a very tough act to follow. Those girls had so much more experience than most of us now. Most of them were two-time Olympians and several-time world competitors. I think there is some pressure to follow their lead, but it is also inspiring. We are a whole new team, so we have to create our own history."

That history would unfold dramatically in 1999 and continue into 2000. But before the final chapter ended, there would be highlights and heartaches, lucky breaks and bone breaks, and more ups and downs than a gymnast's uneven bars routine.

Gymnastics is more than 2,000 years old, but it wasn't until 1924 that the sport became part of the Olympics. Four years later, women gymnasts were allowed to compete for the first time, and in 1936 America fielded a women's gymnastics team. Over the years, women's gymnastics became an important and fan-friendly part of the Olympics, one that would capture the imagination of the public, thanks to the exploits of stars such as Olga Korbut from Belarus (then part of the Soviet Union), Nadia Comaneci from Romania, and an American hero named Mary Lou Retton.

Today, women's gymnastics competitions consist of four extremely demanding and difficult events: vault, uneven bars, balance beam, and floor exercise. Women gymnasts compete not only as a team but also as individuals in event finals, where they attempt to win medals by being the best in each event. Gymnasts also compete in an all-around competition where they try to get the highest combined score in all four events. (For more information on each event and scoring, see "Gymnastics Events and Scoring.")

Europeans dominated the sport for decades. But in 1984 a talented and spunky American teenager named Mary Lou Retton made gymnastics history. Performing in front of a hometown crowd at the Los Angeles Olympics, Mary Lou won the all-around competition and became the first American woman to capture an Olympic gold medal in gymnastics.

Mary Lou also made a huge impression on a whole generation of young gymnasts across the country. Inspired by her gold medal performance, girls jumped into the sport as never before. By the early 1990s, a fresh new cast of talented female gymnasts were ready to make their debut on the national and world stage.

Sure signs that American women were second to none came in 1991, when two-time national champion Kim Zmeskal won the all-around gold medal in the World Championships. Two years later, her teammate Shannon Miller won two individual medals in uneven bars and floor exercise, then took the all-around gold medal as well. In 1994 Miller won the all-around gold medal at the World Championships again. She eventually became the most decorated American gymnast in history, collecting seven Olympic and nine World Championships medals, more than any other American, male or female.

Gymnasts like Miller and Zmeskal may have led the way, but behind them younger and equally talented women were rising through the ranks. In 1994 Dominique Dawes dominated the U.S. National Championships, capturing first place in vault, uneven bars, balance beam, and floor exercise as well as the all-around category. Another American, Dominique Moceanu, won the individual all-around gold medal in 1995. She was just thirteen, the youngest national champion ever.

As the 1996 Olympics in Atlanta approached, the U.S. team was packed with potential and plenty of talent. Gymnastics fans sensed that the time had come for the American women to come into their own, and they were not disappointed. The seven gold medal gymnasts—Shannon Miller, Dominique Dawes, Dominique Moceanu, Kerri Strug, Jaycie Phelps, Amanda Borden, and Amy Chow—became national heroes. They made triumphant appearances in a national tour and on television, and their faces were even featured on millions of Wheaties cereal boxes.

In a sense, the stage was already being set for the 2000 Olympics just a year after the Atlanta Games ended. In 1997, several members of the Magnificent Seven retired, opening the door to some up-and-coming gymnasts who were determined to make their mark on the national scene and on the world stage as well. And since the Summer Games are held only once every four years, the newcomers knew they might get just one chance to compete at the Olympics. For many of them, it would be 2000 or never.

In March 1997, with the memories of the Magnificent Seven still fresh in the minds of gymnastics fans, a new American team, which included several recent graduates of the junior national program, competed at the International Team Championships in Cincinnati, Ohio. The event was a three-way meet between Romania, China, and the United States. In addition to Dominique Moceanu, the American squad included the previous year's junior national champion, fifteen-year-old Vanessa Atler of Canyon Country, California, Jamie Dantzscher, fifteen, from Palmdale, California, and a determined and talented sixteen-year-old from Pen Argyl, Pennsylvania, named Kristen Maloney. Facing the more experienced Chinese and Romanian teams, the Americans finished a respectable second, right behind the Romanians. It was a good sign for the new women's team.

"I think we did very well," Vanessa Atler declared. "There was a great amount of pressure on us because we want to carry the torch of the Mag Seven."

Later in the year, Vanessa Atler used her powerful, aggressive style and amazing athleticism to become the senior co-champion. In

doing so, Vanessa duplicated the feat of
Dominique Moceanu, who in 1995 had also
made the jump from junior to senior national
champion in a single year. Vanessa shared the
title with seventeen-year-old Kristy Powell of
Colorado Springs, Colorado.

Until the final moments of the 1997 U.S.
Gymnastics Championships, Vanessa appeared
to have a lock on the all-around gold. She had
led from the very start, and if she completed
her uneven bars routine without a major mistake, she would have the sole claim on the
gold medal. But in the final rotation, as she
unveiled a new and difficult move called a
Comaneci salto (named after Nadia Comaneci), Vanessa slipped off the uneven bars
and fell. The fall resulted in a reduced score
of 8.650, which allowed Kristy Powell to tie
Vanessa with an identical score of 74.612. It
was the first time in fifteen years there had
been a tie in the event. Sadly for Vanessa
Atler, it would not be the last time that the
uneven bars would prove the undoing of the
young Californian's championship aspirations.

Also in the top ten at the 1997 Nationals
were several other gymnasts destined to be on
the 1999 national team. Kristen Maloney finished fourth, and Jamie Dantzscher, Vanessa

Atler's teammate at the Charter Oak gym in Covina, California, finished sixth. Texas teenager Jennie Thompson placed seventh, and another California teen, Jeanette Antolin from Huntington Beach, rounded out the top ten.

Following the 1997 National Championships, a new American World Championships Team was named. Because of the Magnificent Seven's gold medal performance the year before, expectations for the team were high at the 1997 World Championships held in September in the beautiful alpine city of Lausanne, Switzerland. While Kristy Powell became a member of the Worlds team, Vanessa Atler could not. At fifteen, she was too young under brand-new rules requiring a Worlds competitor to be at least sixteen years old. Vanessa was just forty-eight days short of the minimum age. Fifteen-year-old Jamie Dantzscher also fell victim to the new rule.

The members of the American team—Kendall Beck, Mohini Bhardwaj, Kristen Maloney, Dominique Moceanu, Kristy Powell, and Jennie Thompson—were young and relatively inexperienced. At fifteen, Dominique Moceanu was the youngest but also the most experienced gymnast on the team. Dominique had competed at the 1995 World Championships in Sabae, Japan, under different age-eligibility rules and had been the only woman to win an individual medal—a silver on beam. As a result, she was allowed to go to Lausanne even though she would not be sixteen until the end of September. Kristy Powell was the only other gymnast who had competed in the World Championships.

The American women won their first round, or subdivision, but as the competition continued, the more seasoned European and Chinese teams proved too formidable, and the U.S. team finished sixth. In light of the previous year's events, the American team's showing was disappointing, but there were still reasons for the Americans to cheer. One was provided by Kristen Maloney. In the balance beam segment in the Event Finals, facing world champions such as Russia's Svetlana Khorkina and Romania's Gina Gogean, Kristen scored 9.512, good for seventh place. She was one of only two Americans to place in the top eight in any event. Mohini Bhardwaj of Altamonte Springs, Florida, was the other, placing fifth in the vault.

There were still plenty of hopeful signs on the horizon as another crop of talented and dedicated young women began rising through the ranks. At the 1997 junior nationals, a trio of fifteen-year-olds put on a show. Marline

Stephens of Houston, Texas, was crowned the 1997 national all-around junior champion, followed by Sierra Sapunar of Sebastopol, California. Future 1999 Worlds team member Elise Ray became the junior national champion on uneven bars in 1997, tied for first on balance beam, and won a bronze medal in floor exercise.

In 1998 the American women's team was on the upswing. In March, the U.S. team avenged 1997's second-place finish at the International Team Championships with a great performance in Knoxville, Tennessee. Led by Kristen Maloney, the American women bested strong Romanian and Chinese teams and won the gold medal.

Kristen Maloney saved the day with a cool confidence that would soon become her trademark. The Americans had led from the very start, but began to see their lead slip away late in the competition as several Americans fell off the balance beam. If the Americans were to hold the lead, it was up to Kristen to do her beam routine without a major mistake. Nervous but ready, Kristen reminded herself of the many times she had done solid beam sets in practice. This time would be no different. She came to the rescue with a 9.800 score, which gave the Americans an even bigger lead.

Then Kristen followed that with a 9.800 on the floor exercise, ensuring the U.S. victory. Kristen won the all-around gold, took first in beam and floor exercise, and placed third in vault.

"We all knew Kristen could pull through for us," a happy Vanessa Atler said afterward. Kristen herself would describe the moment as "the best feeling I ever had."

It was an impressive victory for the young Americans. In July, at the Pacific Alliance Championships, a competition between countries bordering the Pacific Ocean, Kristen and Vanessa teamed up to lead the Americans to gold. Kristen ignored a painful stress fracture in her right shin and won the all-around gold, while Vanessa claimed gold medals in vault and floor exercise. Together the pair led the Americans to the team gold as well. This event was important for two reasons: it was a qualifying event for the more important Pan Am Games to be held in Canada the following year, and it would provide momentum for another important event, the Goodwill Games, in New York in July.

The gold rush continued at the Goodwill Games, and it proved beyond any doubt that the U.S. women's team could stand toe-to-toe with their international counterparts. Dominique Moceanu provided the highlights this time. Although she had won a silver medal in floor exercise at the 1997 Nationals, the former national champion had not been performing at the level she had reached in 1994–1995. Dominique, it seemed, also had a tough act to follow—herself.

At the Goodwill Games, Dominique made a dramatic comeback by outperforming three-time world champion Svetlana Khorkina of Russia and winning the all-around title, despite a bad cold. It was the first time a non-Russian had won the all-around at that event. It was such a dramatic moment that Dominique broke down and cried tears of joy as she accepted her gold medal.

The Americans also took three out of the four gold medals awarded in the Event Finals, Kristen Maloney placed first on beam, and Vanessa Atler won the gold in vault and floor exercise, where she outperformed Romanian star Simona Amanar. Even then, Sydney in 2000 was on Vanessa's mind.

"I expected to medal," Vanessa said confidently, "but I wasn't sure, especially since Simona Amanar did a really great routine. This is a good confidence builder for the Sydney Olympic Games and the upcoming U.S. Championships."

The 1998 U.S. Gymnastics Championships

in Indianapolis was expected to be a battle of champions. Vanessa Atler was expected to take sole possession of the title of U.S. champion, but she would face stiff competition from past champs Dominique Moceanu and Kim Zmeskal. Kristen Maloney was ready to make a bid for the title, too.

Unfortunately for Vanessa Atler, the uneven bars jinx struck again. During the preliminary round of the all-around competition, she fell off the uneven bars doing her Comaneci salto once again. Her low 8.225 score allowed a steady and consistent Kristen Maloney to outscore Vanessa and take the title. Vanessa settled for silver and Dominique Moceanu, competing with a sore left knee, took the bronze. Jennie Thompson and Elise Ray rounded out the top five.

Vanessa redeemed herself in the Event Finals, winning the floor exercise gold with a beautiful routine that earned a 9.850, the highest score of the competition. Dominique Moceanu won the gold medal in vault and beam, and Elise Ray became the new uneven bars champion with a superb performance that earned a 9.825 score.

The 1998 Nationals introduced some new talent, too. Alyssa Beckerman of Middletown, New Jersey, won the silver on uneven bars, and Jeanette Antolin won the bronze. Jamie Dantzscher won the silver in floor exercise. Morgan White, a determined fifteen-year-old from Florida, was crowned the new junior national champion.

The 1998 National Championships clearly established Kristen as the best female gymnast in America. "I'm really excited and I'm kind of speechless," she said after accepting her gold medal. "I don't know what to say or think. I'm so happy. I didn't really think of beating anyone. I just thought about going out there and doing my best." Even more amazing was the fact that Kristen had won despite a painful stress fracture in her shinbone.

"I was a little worried about [the fracture] going into the competition," she admitted afterward, "but once the adrenaline kicked in, I forgot all about it." That kind of steely determination and resolve had carried Kristen to her first national title. Those qualities would soon bring her even greater success.

The 1998 U.S. Gymnastics championships were also a turning point for Elise Ray, the new uneven bars champion. It was her first major meet as a senior, and her grace and elegance impressed all those who saw her.

As the 1998 season ended, the American women were looking ahead to 1999, the final season before the millennium and the 2000 Olympics. But if 1996 marked the coming of age of American women's gymnastics, 1999 would soon demonstrate that the sport was about to go through some major growing pains, both literally and figuratively. The road to Sydney beckoned, but plenty of bumps and obstacles lay ahead, as the team would soon find out.

On the World Stage

As the 1999 season started, the race toward Sydney began to heat up. National and World Championships take on added significance in a pre-Olympics year. As Tim Daggett, an NBC commentator and a bronze medal winner at the 1984 Olympics noted, "The final lap bell always rings one year before the Olympic Games."

Although the national team lacked the experience and leadership of Mag Seven stars such as Shannon Miller, Dominique Dawes, and Kerri Strug, there were many reasons for optimism. They included the emergence of Kristen Maloney and Elise Ray, the experience of Jennie Thompson, and the tremendous potential of Vanessa Atler, who despite her bad luck on bars, clearly had the talent to be among the world's best. There were also new faces such as Sierra Sapunar and 1998 junior nationals champ Morgan White, who was now ready to compete as a senior. Alyssa Beckerman, Jamie Dantzscher, and Jeanette Antolin had all gained valuable experience and were eager to show what they could do, too.

The new season got under way in sunny Pomona, California in February at the American Classic meet. The event also served as a qualifier for the Pan Am Games in Winnipeg, Canada, an important international competition scheduled for July. Only the top six American women would earn the trip to Winnipeg.

Vanessa Atler reinforced her reputation as a powerhouse performer as she ran away with the competition, winning all four events with scores of 9.825 or better in vault, beam, and floor. Her combined score was more than a point and a half higher than that of her nearest rival, Jennie Thompson. Kristen Maloney, Elise Ray, and several other notable gymnasts sat out the meet because of injuries or illness, but third-place finisher Alyssa Beckerman, Jeanette Antolin, Jamie Dantzscher, and Erinn Dooley all qualified for the Pan Am Games. A disappointed Morgan White finished seventh, one spot shy of qualifying.

Jennie Thompson continued to shine as she won the American Cup event in Saint Petersburg, Florida, in March. Facing a field of talented international gymnasts, Thompson took the gold while Vanessa Atler continued her medal-winning ways by taking a bronze in the all-around. Vanessa would have finished higher had it not been for a shaky bars set.

Later that month, Vanessa traveled to Paris, France, for the French Telecom meet. She was steady on uneven bars but suffered a mishap during the floor routine, normally one of her best events. During a tumbling pass, she took a bad fall, and when she got up, she clutched her ankle in pain. She shrugged it off, but later it was revealed that she had bruised the ankle badly. The injury didn't receive much attention at the time, but it would have fateful consequences for Vanessa at the National and World Championships later that year

While Vanessa Atler would be briefly sidelined by her sore ankle, Kristen Maloney was back in action by late March as the 1999 International Team Championships got under way. The Americans squared off against teams from China, Australia, and Romania, home of the current world champions, whose star Simona Amanar was the defending world champion.

The Romanians overpowered the other three teams, edging out the United States for the gold by a little more than half a point.

Kristen Maloney won the vault event and
scored 9.675 on bars, 9.650 on beam, and 9.72
on floor, but Amanar led her team to the gold.
Jennie Thompson and Alyssa Beckerman finished sixth and seventh in the all-around, and
Elise Ray's strong 9.8 scores on uneven bars
were a highlight of the meet.

Two weeks later, a U.S. women's team con-
sisting of Morgan White, Kim Zmeskal, Jamie
Dantzscher, Tasha Schwikert, Angela Beam,
and Audra Fraim, took on the Chinese national
team in a two-country meet. Morgan White was
particularly impressive, competing in all four
events, scoring a 9.5 on floor and beam, and 9.7
on bars. Late in the competition the Chinese
team took the lead. The outcome of the meet
now hinged on Morgan's performance on vault.
She needed a 9.312 just to tie the Chinese.
Instead she scored a 9.5, and the U.S. women
edged out the Chinese, 113.462 to 113.274.

The Pan Am Games, which pitted the United
States against teams from Canada, Cuba, and
several South American countries, were usually
seen as a showcase for American athletes. As
the favorites, the Americans were hoping to win
the team gold, and team captain Jennie Thompson was favored in the all-around. However,
without Vanessa Atler and Kristen Maloney,
who were sitting out the competition, the team

was not at full strength. But because of Vanessa's withdrawal, Morgan White would now get to compete, and she was thrilled.

Unfortunately for the Americans, there was good news and bad news. The bad news was that their early lead slipped away following a series of mistakes and falls off the balance beam. Seizing the opportunity, a talented Canadian team grabbed the gold. The Americans had to be content with the silver medal.

"We could give a busload of excuses," said American coach Mary Lee Tracy, "but we just got beat today."

The good news was provided by the youngest member of the U.S. squad. Morgan White, who had just turned sixteen the month before, surprised nearly everyone with a gold medal performance in the all-around. Prior to the meet, coach Mary Lee Tracy had told Morgan that if she did her best and kept her confidence up, she had a shot at the gold. Still, Morgan was a bit anxious. "I was nervous coming into the games," Morgan confessed later, "because it is a big meet with gymnasts I have never competed against, plus I am the youngest." Cool and competent, Morgan was solid in all four events, and when the leader, Michelle Conway of Canada, fell off the beam in her final rotation, Morgan took sole possession of first place. She also picked up a bronze medal on bars, making her the only American woman to win an individual medal. It was a tremendous confidence booster for the young gymnast. "I couldn't feel better going into the Nationals now," she said.

Magnificent Seven member Shannon Miller, who'd won the all-around gold in the 1995 Pan Am Games, was in the audience. Like many spectators, she was impressed by Morgan's performance. Later she said that Morgan reminded her of another gymnast—herself.

Jennie Thompson had a shot at the gold in the all-around, but bobbled a bit on beam, which dropped her into third place. Worse, she injured her ankle during her vault in the Event Finals and had to withdraw from the competition. The ankle would bother her for the rest of the season.

Injuries continued to narrow the field as the 1999 Nationals approached. The 1998 junior vault champion Angela Beam dislocated an elbow early, and Kim Zmeskal tore an Achilles tendon. Mag Seven gymnast Amy Chow suffered an ankle injury, and Dominique Moceanu was plagued by back and knee problems. The talent pool for the 2000 Olympics seemed to be getting shallower by the week.

Gymnastics is as risky and as physically demanding as any sport. The constant stress from high-flying dismounts, flips, and other high-impact moves inevitably takes a toll on a gymnast's body. Injuries are a fact of life in the sport, even though gymnasts are among the most perfectly conditioned, well-muscled, and agile of athletes. "It's part of the sport," says Kristen Maloney. "You know it's a risk factor. All you can do is keep your conditioning up and stay strong."

In August, the U.S. Classic meet took place. It was the final women's qualifying event for the 1999 U.S. Gymnastics Championships, scheduled to take place later that month in Sacramento, California. Sierra Sapunar, who had recently recovered from a broken foot, won her first title as a senior, taking the all-around gold at the Classic. But bad luck struck a few weeks later as Sierra suffered a freak accident while training on the uneven bars. Falling stiff-armed off the bars, she dislocated her shoulder and chipped a bone in her elbow, putting her on the sidelines, too.

Still, Kristen Maloney, Vanessa Atler, Elise Ray, Morgan White, and a host of other young hopefuls were ready and eager to vie for the national title at the upcoming Nationals. The event was the next stepping-stone on the path to Sydney, and it was shaping up to be quite a showdown.

The Showdown in Sacramento

Pressure and excitement began building early as the 1999 Nationals neared. *USA Today* quoted Nadia Comaneci and others saying that Vanessa Atler was poised to be the next gymnastics superstar, the next Mary Lou Retton. Others saw defending national champion Kristen Maloney as America's leading gymnast. While the two gymnasts were good friends off the floor, their competitiveness did create a strong and healthy rivalry on the floor.

Even though Kristen Maloney was defending champion, Vanessa Atler was ranked number one based on her earlier 1999 scores. Because she had sat out the early part of the season with her sore shin, Kristen was currently ranked number eleven, and to some she was the underdog. Kristen would have to be in top form—or Vanessa Atler would have to be in less than first-place form—to keep her title. And none of the girls heading to Sacramento needed to be reminded that because of the upcoming Olympics, the 1999 Nationals took on even greater significance than usual.

"This is where we start fulfilling dreams and breaking hearts," said coach Mary Lee Tracy. The annual U.S. Gymnastics Championships meet is the most important national meet of the season, and many gymnasts train all year for it. In a pre-Olympics year, the Nationals can play a very significant role in picking the potential Olympians.

There were many questions as the championships began. Could Kristen Maloney overcome the painful stress fracture in her leg and keep her national title? Would Vanessa Atler put her uneven bars problems behind her and use her considerable skills and power to reclaim the title, as so many said she could? Or would another up-and-coming gymnast pull off an upset? Elise Ray, 1998 uneven bars champion, had shown great promise recently. With beautiful lines and graceful dance-like moves, she was described by one longtime observer as "poetry in motion." The presence of veterans like Jennie Thompson, Jamie

Dantzscher, Jeanette Antolin, and Alyssa Beckerman, in addition to relative newcomer Morgan White, who was brimming with confidence following her triumph at the 1999 Pan Am Games, promised to make the 1999 Nationals an especially thrilling event.

"A lot of kids have the chance to walk through a big open door," noted Mary Lee Tracy, coach of several top-ranked gymnasts, including Alyssa Beckerman, Jennie Thompson, and Morgan White.

There are a lot of gymnastics fans in California, and 25,000 of them came to Sacramento's Arco Arena for the four-day meet. After Kristen Maloney's dramatic upset over Vanessa Atler in 1998, fans knew anything could happen. Kristen and Vanessa knew it, too. "I'm a little nervous, about the pressure, about defending, about the way I'm working out right now," Kristen Maloney admitted prior to the competition. Because of her shin, she hadn't competed since March. "I did it last summer with a hurt leg and won the national championship, so I ought to be able to do it again," Kristen declared.

Vanessa Atler was not at full strength either. Her ankle had been bothering her since the March meet in France. From the first rotation, the all-around competition was a close battle.

An anxious Kristen Maloney began with a solid routine on bars, which earned her a 9.575, but Vanessa matched her score with her beam routine. Vanessa dazzled the crowd in her next event, floor exercise, using her impressive tumbling and acrobatic skills, along with expressive dance-like movements to score a 9.85, the best score of the evening. Kristen watched Vanessa finish her floor exercise, then turned in a solid beam set to earn a 9.575.

The third rotation was thrilling as Vanessa performed a spectacular double-twisting vault and stuck (made a perfect landing in which the performer's feet seem to stick to the mat) to collect a 9.712 score. Waiting on the sidelines, Kristen heard the crowd cheer loudly for Vanessa's vault score. Unfazed, she turned in a superb floor exercise program set to music from *West Side Story* and earned a 9.800.

As the final rotation began, Vanessa had a tiny .037 lead. Her final event would be bars. Everyone in the arena seemed to be focused on the young California teenager—everyone, that is, except Kristen Maloney, who found it too suspenseful to watch. Instead, she sipped ice water and tried to concentrate on her final event, vault.

The crowd was subdued as Vanessa began, many wondering if she would successfully complete her trademark move, the Comaneci salto, which had given her so much trouble in the past. The Comaneci salto is a very difficult move which requires a gymnast to move from the low bar to the high bar by reaching between her legs to grab the high bar and then flip over it. Twice during warm-ups, Vanessa had done it successfully. Just moments later, as a crowd of nearly 8,000 watched intently, she attempted it.

Kristen Maloney, still avoiding looking at Vanessa, heard the crowd let out a loud collective gasp.

As she tried to complete the Comaneci salto, Vanessa seemed to have trouble with her release. As she reached for the high bar, she lost her grip and fell. She got up quickly and completed her routine with a spectacular full twisting double layout, but her 9.125 score was not good enough to keep her in first place. A mistake-free bars set would, in all likelihood, have won the title for Vanessa. Instead, her 9.125 score had opened the door for Kristen who, despite her nervousness, was prepared as usual to walk right through it.

Kristen, knowing the final score would be close, told herself to relax. She tried to ignore Vanessa's score and reminded herself how she had nailed her vaults in practice. "Go hard and land," she said to herself. Ignoring her sore shin, Kristen nailed her two vaults, stuck both landings, and scored a solid 9.587.

Kristen won the all around by three-tenths of a point. Once again, her steadiness and consistency, combined with Vanessa Atler's fall, had made Kristen the national champion. Vanessa took the silver, and Jennie Thompson won the bronze medal. Alyssa Beckerman, Jamie Dantzscher, and Elise Ray completed the top six.

"I tried to go out tonight and do the best I could, but I was really nervous on bars," Kristen said afterward. "I thought my beam routine was the best I have ever done, so I am very proud of my performance." In her usual fashion, Kristen made light of her sore shin. "It was pretty sore during morning workout, but during meets it kind of goes away. I try not to think about it. With all the adrenaline it sort of takes a backseat, and I don't really feel it that much. I just tried to focus on my vault and what I had to do."

"Yes, I did it again," Vanessa Atler told reporters. "People keep telling me to change my bars, but . . . that's my bar routine and I'm going to keep it.

"Yeah, I'm disappointed," she admitted. "I wanted to win and thought I could do it. But

for some reason I wasn't ready. I hadn't competed in a while because of my ankle and for
some reason, I was scared tonight. I guess I
didn't want it bad enough." Vanessa shrugged
and smiled. "I make it all the time in practice,
but when I go out in the meet, it gets harder
or something. I guess I think about it too
much."

After the excitement of the all-around competition, Event Finals were a bit anticlimactic.
This time it was Kristen Maloney who struggled on bars and fell, ending up last in the
event. She finished second on vault, and sat
out the floor exercise and beam events to save
her sore shin for the upcoming World Championships. Both Jennie Thompson and Jamie
Dantzscher withdrew from the vault, while
Vanessa Atler skipped floor exercise because
of her sore ankle.

Still, the Event Finals were Vanessa's show
this time. Cheered on by the supportive California crowd, she turned in an excellent beam
routine that earned the gold medal. She also
finished first in vault. However, being named
national champion in two events was not
enough to ease her earlier disappointment. "It
helps," she said, "but it doesn't make up for
the other night. It does make me feel a little
better."

On the uneven bars Jennie Thompson and Jamie Dantzscher received identical 9.675 scores and shared the gold. Morgan White and Alyssa Beckerman tied for third, scoring 9.550. Jennie Thompson also picked up a bronze on the beam.

The new floor exercise champion was Elise Ray. Her elegant and expressive moves and near-perfect tumbling and acrobatic flips earned her a 9.775 and the gold medal. Morgan White, bouncing back from her seventh-place all-around showing, picked up the silver medal.

Prior to Nationals, Elise Ray had been described as a "dance-only" gymnast, one who emphasized a balletic approach rather than a spectacular acrobatic style. With Vanessa Atler absent from the floor exercise finals, Elise received a lot of attention and impressed everyone with her grace and sophistication. The performance also demonstrated how confident she had become and just how much her skills had grown.

Vanessa Atler, on the other hand, was experiencing some moments of doubt. "I just have to continue to believe in myself," she said. But after Sacramento, Vanessa's mother, Nanette, told reporters, "We're going back to the drawing board. We might make some changes."

Most people assumed that meant changes in her bars program. Instead, Vanessa surprised the gymnastics world by announcing that she would be leaving her longtime coaches, Beth and Steve Rybacki, with whom she'd trained for six years. Vanessa explained in her on-line diary that with the approaching Worlds and Olympics—perhaps the most important competitions of her career—the time had come to make some changes in her routines and training.

The World Team Trials, another important pre-Olympics event, began in Kansas City, Missouri, on September 15, 1999. Sixteen of the top-ranked male and female gymnasts were invited to compete for a place on the team heading to Tianjin, China, and the 1999 World Championships. Only six gymnasts would qualify for each team.

Magnificent Seven member Amy Chow, who was trying to make a comeback from ankle surgery, was one of the hopefuls. So was Jeanette Antolin, who had missed the 1999 Nationals because of a sore neck. Also vying for a place on the women's team were Elise Ray, Jamie Dantzscher, Alyssa Beckerman, Morgan White, and Angela Beam. Kristen Maloney and Vanessa Atler were sitting out the trials because of injuries, but they had already successfully petitioned their way onto the Worlds team. So only four spots were left on the women's team. A fifth gymnast would be selected as an alternate. The competition promised to be intense.

Jennie Thompson was the leader after the preliminary round, with Elise Ray just .21 points behind her. Alyssa Beckerman was in third place.

Acute sinusitis soon forced Jennie Thompson to withdraw from the trials, but based on her scores from earlier in the season, she too was able to petition her way onto the Worlds team. Only three spots and an alternate position were open now.

Elise Ray took the lead and put on one of the most impressive shows of her career. She turned in a stunning and polished set on uneven bars and showed marked improvement and increased difficulty levels in her other events. Jeanette Antolin, known for her originality, style, and presence, drew loud cheers when she unveiled her new floor exercise routine, which was set to music from *Gone With the Wind*. Her bars routine also featured a new impressive move, a layout Jaeger, which boosted her scores. Jeanette's performance earned her a second-place finish and a spot on the Worlds team.

The end of the trials turned into a suspenseful nail-biter between Alyssa Beckerman in third place and Jamie Dantzscher in fourth. Alyssa was nursing a sore wrist, but had managed to take a small lead in time for the final and decisive event—beam. The pressure was intense. As she performed on the 4-inch-wide beam, Alyssa seemed to be in total control and was doing beautifully. Then she suddenly slipped and fell. Looking stunned and dazed, she jumped back on and finished her routine. Her score was announced: 8.825.

Jamie Dantzscher now had a chance to overtake her teammate, and she started strong in her beam routine. But during a tricky flip-flop with full tuck (see Glossary), she lost her balance, too. She began flailing her arms furiously, trying to stay on. She did and was able to finish her routine with no further mishaps. Her score was 9.05.

At first it appeared that Jamie had edged out Alyssa for the final spot on the team, and Jamie's coaches, Beth and Steve Rybacki, happily hugged her. When the final scores were announced, however, joy turned to disappointment. Alyssa's total score was still .13 points higher. She would be the final team member, while Jamie would have to settle for alternate.

Magnificent Seven member Amy Chow,

whose ankle had given her trouble throughout the trials, finished out of the running in fourteenth place. For Pan Am gold medalist Morgan White, there were only tears. She finished fifth, just missing the alternate position. She cried as her coach, Mary Lee Tracy, hugged her and tried to console her.

The World Team Trials were a milestone for Elise Ray. Her performance put her on the cover of *USA Gymnastics* magazine with the caption "Ray of Hope." "I felt really prepared, and that boosted my confidence," Elise said modestly. "I'm so excited to be here for the first time."

Jeanette Antolin, too, was thrilled with her performance. "I was proud of my floor," she said. "This is only the second time I've done my floor routine, and it took all my adrenaline. At the 1997 Worlds I was an alternate. It was a disappointment because I had to watch from the stands. Now I'm just so excited that I get to go and actually compete. It's a dream come true."

Alyssa Beckerman, unfortunately, was about to have her dreams dashed. A week after the trials, X-rays revealed that the soreness in her wrist was really a tiny fracture. Amazed Alyssa had been able to compete at the trials at all, doctors recommended that she withdraw from the Worlds team. "It's just better for her not to risk six months out of the gym," Alyssa's coach, Mary Lee Tracy, said with obvious disappointment.

In sports, one person's bad luck can turn into someone else's big break, and that proved true for both Jamie Dantzscher and Morgan White. When Alyssa Beckerman withdrew from the Worlds team, Jamie became a full competing member of the team and Morgan White moved up to alternate. "I'm really excited about being an alternate on the Worlds team," Morgan said, "but I wish it hadn't been at the expense of my teammate, Alyssa."

At the end of September, the new Worlds team headed to the Parkettes Training Center in Allentown, Pennsylvania, Kristen Maloney's home gym, to prepare for the World Championships under the guidance of Kristen's coach, Donna Strauss. The young women on the team enjoyed being in each other's company for the week. Several were already close friends as a result of the experiences they had shared at earlier meets. As the Worlds approached, the six gymnasts developed a solid team spirit and a close camaraderie.

"I feel this is going to be a really strong team, and that we're going to pull together and do really well at Worlds," Kristen Maloney predicted with her characteristic confidence. "I think we have a good chance of medaling as long as we stay focused, stay together, cheer each other on, and hit our routines."

The Americans' aspirations were modest. They hoped to finish third as a team and perhaps win a medal or two in individual competition. One problem the team would face at the Worlds was that international judges would probably be tougher on the Americans than judges at home. At the end of the World Team Trials, coach Donna Strauss predicted, "Wait till the World Championships. The scoring there will be tough." The team would soon find just how prophetic Strauss's comment would turn out to be.

Some of the Americans' routines featured moves that were less difficult than those of some of the Europeans, so their start values (the assigned value of a move from which points are added or deducted) would be lower. That in turn could lead to lower overall scores.

The team was hobbled further when Jennie Thompson once again injured her left ankle during a practice vault just days before the competition. Doctors told her the injury was severe enough to prevent her from competing at the Worlds. Alternate Morgan White took her place and would now be able to compete.

The 34th World Artistic Gymnastics Championships competition was held in Tianjin, a port city of 9 million residents on the east coast of China. This too was an important qualifying event for the Sydney Olympics. Only the top twelve teams would send full squads to the Games, while the rest of the countries would be limited to individual competitors. More than 650 gymnasts from seventy countries, including the top-ranked Russians, Romanians, and Chinese, were expected to compete.

The 1999 Worlds also happened to coincide with the fiftieth anniversary of the People's Republic of China. It was also the first time China, a country with a long and proud gymnastics history, had hosted such an event. As a result, Tianjin was gripped by gymnastics fever and the meet organizers rolled out the red carpet. Arriving gymnasts were greeted by large welcoming signs and huge neon displays in the shape of performing gymnasts. Brightly colored flags, banners, and balloons fluttered in the autumn breeze. Outside the 10,000-seat Tianjin Gymnasium, local bands, traditional dance troupes, and tiny gymnasts, none older than seven, entertained the visitors.

The spectacular opening ceremonies drew thousands of spectators who cheered loudly as flag-waving teams paraded by. Fans clamored to catch a glimpse of gymnastics superstars like the current world champions Svetlana Khorkina of Russia and Ivan Ivankov of Belarus.

The United States team was young and relatively inexperienced compared to the team that had competed in 1997. Of the six team members, only Kristen Maloney had competed in an earlier Worlds. All the Americans were keenly aware of the importance of the meet. Elise Ray and Jeanette Antolin had competed in China before, but not at the Worlds level. "The feeling before the competition was very intense and very nerve-racking," Elise Ray would say later. "I think it really helped me having been to China before and experiencing all the differences."

In the women's team preliminaries, the Americans had mixed results. The team got off to a good start on vault with no one scoring lower than a 9.299. While Vanessa performed her bars set without a mistake, however, Kristen Maloney fell the wrong way on a handstand and struggled with her dismount, earning a lower-than-usual 8.975. Elise Ray gave the team a boost with a 9.6 bars score, but Jamie Dantzscher lost her grip on the lower bar and scored 8.312 on bars. Morgan

White fell during her beam routine, and Jeanette Antolin had some wobbly moments, too, but managed to avoid falling. Vanessa Atler was in good form on beam and landed her double tuck dismount perfectly, scoring 9.612. A steady Kristen Maloney came through with an identical 9.612 score.

But with only one event—floor exercise—to go, it suddenly seemed possible that the U.S. team might not make it to the finals. Only the top six teams would qualify. The Romanian, Russian, Chinese, and Ukrainian teams seemed assured of a place in the finals, but the United States, Australia, and Spain were locked in a battle for the two final spots. Luckily, floor exercise was one of the Americans' strongest events.

Elise Ray contributed a polished and precise routine that earned a 9.612. Jamie Dantzscher and Jeanette Antolin scored 9.137 and 9.262, respectively, while Kristen Maloney gave an inspired performance that garnered a 9.750. Vanessa, the final American in the event, offered a beautiful routine, then landed a triple twist dismount that received a 9.762, the Americans' top score in any event. Vanessa's floor score put the team three-tenths of a point ahead of the Australians, who edged out the Spanish for the sixth spot in the finals.

Vanessa was the seventh finisher overall,

with Elise Ray in twelfth place. Kristen's lower-than-usual bars score resulted in her finishing in sixteenth place. "I feel great," Vanessa Atler exulted. "I was a little nervous and not sure how we'd do, but I think we all did great. We were just scared. We were nervous about making the top six, and we know we can go out there and win a medal now."

"I definitely think we can win a team medal," Elise Ray agreed. "We are a really good group that works well together. We have a lot to learn from this World Championships, but also a lot to gain from it."

One main difference between the 1999 Worlds and other major meets was that there was no live TV coverage. Since competitors would not have to wait while TV crews set up and moved around, the pace was fast and frantic, with four events going on at the same time and gymnasts performing constantly. That would prove to be particularly true during the women's team finals.

In the finals, the Americans were solid but not spectacular on vault as Vanessa Atler and Kristen Maloney contributed high marks of 9.599 and 9.424. Except for Elise Ray who had a team-best score of 9.725, none of the other girls scored higher than 9.250. But no one made any major mistakes, either.

As the Americans prepared for the balance beam, the Chinese team suddenly rallied and the hometown crowd grew louder and rowdier. Several Chinese fans began racing around the arena, waving flags and cheering loudly. Some of them even screamed "Fall, fall," in Chinese when foreign gymnasts had a shaky moment on bars and beam. More than a few of the gymnasts appeared to be distracted by the noise and the fast-paced proceedings.

Vanessa Atler, already somewhat nervous, appeared to be one of them. Normally steady on beam, Vanessa fell off, not once but twice. Kristen Maloney, known for her unshakable concentration and focus, ignored the crowd and delivered an error-free beam routine that was awarded a 9.550. Despite Kristen's solid score, however, the American team's hopes for a medal were slipping away.

Later an embarrassed Vanessa Atler would say of her beam routine, "It was the most nervous I have ever been in my entire life. I don't know what happened. The crowd was really loud, and that was hard."

Floor exercises also proved to be a problem, although that wasn't the fault of the gymnasts. When Jeanette Antolin was ready to begin her floor exercises, meet organizers couldn't find the right music. It took three attempts and five minutes to start her music. Jeanette completed her routine without further incident, but Jamie Dantzscher stepped out of bounds in what had been an otherwise strong showing. Kristen Maloney was halfway though an outstanding performance when her music suddenly stopped right before her final tumbling pass. Cool and collected, Kristen finished her routine without music, and earned a 9.662, but coach Kelli Hill was furious. "They turned it off," she yelled with disbelief. "They turned off [Maloney's] music, and they put up the wrong music [for Jeanette Antolin]. To turn off an athlete's music is inexcusable."

Vanessa Atler regained her composure in the floor exercise and earned a 9.512. Elise Ray again earned the team's highest score, 9.725, but it was not enough to boost the American team's total above a sixth-place finish. The Romanians, led by Maria Olaru and Simona Amanar, took the gold, followed by Russia, China, Ukraine, and Australia.

The news got worse as the Event Finals arrived. During a practice session, Kristen Maloney missed a move and hit her knee on the uneven bars as she crashed to the floor. Doctors examined her injured knee and decided that she would not be able to compete in the all-around or the Event Finals.

Except for Elise Ray, the Event Finals were a letdown for the Americans. Facing formidable competition on the uneven bars from Svetlana Khorkina, and Huang Mandan and Ling Jie of China, Elise turned in a flowing, in-control performance that earned a 9.637 score, good for seventh place. She was the only American to finish in the top eight in any event.

Vanessa Atler struggled with her bars set and had a disastrous floor exercise routine in which she landed awkwardly and nearly had to reach down to the floor to keep her balance. Her score was a crushing 7.9. Even worse, she reinjured her ankle during the performance.

Elise Ray again provided the only bright spot in the all-around by finishing eighth. Vanessa Atler ended up in thirty-first place.

The U.S. team members were clearly dissatisfied with their finish, but they tried to put the best face on their performance. Vanessa Atler explained that the Tianjin Worlds were a challenge, not only because of the level of competition but also because of the noise and the fast-paced proceedings. "Most of us have never been to a World Championship before and [had to] deal with some of this stuff," she elaborated. "We are not saying we didn't make mistakes. We did, but when things like that happen it's hard to get your mind off of it. You've just got to learn from it and not be so nervous next time."

"It just wasn't there tonight," Kristen Maloney added. "Hopefully we can come back next year."

Elise Ray, who had the most to be happy about, saw reasons to be optimistic. "This has been an exciting experience. It's quite a feeling to be in the same arena with the best in the world. You really can't know about it until you are out there, and I want to do it all over again.

"I think we did a great job as a team," she added. "There were a lot of distractions and things that we weren't expecting. But overall we stayed determined on what we had to do. It's all a learning experience."

"These girls are a great group of fighters. I'm proud to be on the floor with them," Elise's coach, Kelli Hill, asserted. "We'll keep training and we'll be more ready for Sydney," she promised.

AMERICAN GYMNASTS CLOSE-UPS:
Kristen Maloney

Cool, confident, and consistent. Those are the hallmarks of Kristen Maloney's gymnastics career. National champion in 1998 and 1999, Kristen is one of America's best hopes for an Olympic medal. She's a natural leader who inspires her teammates and has won the hearts of countless gymnastics fans. While other gymnasts have occasionally folded in the face of pressure, Kristen is known for her unshakable concentration and single-minded determination to succeed.

In 1997, Kristen was ranked fourteenth in the country. The next year she rose to fourth, and in 1998 Kristen captured the all-around title for the first time. She did it again in 1999 despite a painful stress fracture in her shin. Not many gymnasts can match Kristen's stamina, strength, and self-confidence.

While her teammates admit feeling the pressure to live up to the achievements of the Magnificent Seven, Kristen dismisses comparisons with that legendary team. "We are not the Magnificent Seven," Kristen asserted in her usual forthright manner. "I don't feel we have to show anybody that we are as good as them; we just have to do as well as we know we can."

Kristen Ann Maloney was born on March 10, 1981, in Hackettstown, New Jersey. She's the third of three children born to Rich and Linda Maloney. The family currently lives in Pen Argyl, a small town in Pennsylvania that Kristen has put on the map with her success.

Kristen's name has sometimes been spelled "Kristin." Her birth certificate has "in," but when she first learned to spell her name, she always wrote it with an "en," and that version stuck. Kristen finds either spelling acceptable.

She was always a very active child. "My mom said I was always jumping on things," Kristen said. When her parents enrolled her older brother Shawn and sister Carrie in gymnastics classes, five-year-old Kristen wanted to go with them, so her mother signed her up for lessons too.

Kristen tried other sports but preferred gymnastics. "I guess I have always liked gymnastics," she recalled. "I can't remember not liking it. After a while, I got more serious about it. I would pick gymnastics over other sports I tried. I guess it was because it was the most fun, and also I could go year-round, unlike the other sports I played. Gymnastics slowly became a large part of my life."

She started out at a small New Jersey gym and then, at age seven, joined the International Gymnastics club in Stroudsburg, Pennsylvania. But the gym did not have a strong girls' program, so Kristen moved to Bill and Donna Strauss's Parkettes Training Center in Allentown, Pennsylvania. She has been with Parkettes ever since.

Her first and biggest gymnastics hero was Nadia Comaneci, whose power and grace impressed young Kristen every time she saw her perform on videos and TV. Later she would be inspired by Dominique Dawes.

Kristen was competing on an international level by the time she was twelve. She had a spectacular start in 1993 when she traveled to England to compete in the Heathrow Gold Cup. She won the all-around and captured first place in both beam and vault, but in 1994 she tore a triceps muscle. Although she won several medals in international meets that year, she was not at full strength when she competed as a senior at the 1995 National Championships. She finished a disappointing twenty-sixth.

After that, she worked even harder, and at the 1996 Nationals, fifteen-year-old Kristen finished just out of medal contention with a fourth place in floor exercise, her favorite event. Her performance in the all-around competition was good enough (fourteenth) to qualify her for the Olympic team trials, but faced with competition from the Magnificent Seven, she didn't make the team.

Like her 1999 Worlds teammates, Kristen watched the 1996 Olympics on TV at home and dreamed of getting her chance. She was thrilled when the Americans won the gold medal. "I was happy for them," she remembered. "I was really excited. But it kind of got me down, too, because that could have been me. You don't want to think like that too long. And I knew there would always be 2000."

The year 1997 marked a coming-out for the sixteen-year-old gymnast. Early in the year she won a gold medal in the all-around at the American Classic in New Haven, Connecticut. In March, with Vanessa Atler on the sidelines, Kristen unveiled a new floor exercise routine and placed second in the all-around to lead the U.S. team to a second-place finish behind Romania at the International Team Championships in Richmond, Virginia. She gave an impressive performance at the 1997 Nationals, taking a silver in vault and a bronze in floor exercise, and placing fifth in beam. She might have won the all-around had it not been for two falls during her bars set.

"I was frustrated on bars because I fell both days," she admitted. "It really kind of upset me because I knew I could do it. I had it in the back of my head that it was going to be a problem, so I was really getting nervous on bars. And it usually isn't a problem during workouts. It's just when I go into competitions that I get more nervous."

The 1997 World Championships in Lausanne, Switzerland, were a huge confidence booster for Kristen, although when she first got out on the floor with the world's best gymnasts—girls she had seen only on TV until then—she was totally taken aback. Regaining her composure, she anchored the Americans' efforts and helped the team take sixth place.

She qualified for the Event Finals in beam, and if she was nervous before the competition, she grew even more uneasy as she waited for the first gymnast, Romania's Gina Gogean, to start. Gogean was supremely confident, and with two golds at the previous year's Worlds, she had good reason to be. The Romanian star shocked the crowd at the Malley Sports Center—and the gymnasts who had to follow her—with a superb vault that was scored at 9.8. With five gymnasts scheduled to vault ahead of her, the pressure and tension level instantly doubled for Kristen.

It was, as Kristen later put it, "shocking to see Gogean get such a high score right out of the gate." However, Kristen took a deep breath and told herself to just go out and do her best. She delivered a solid beam routine that earned a 9.512 score. It was not enough to win a medal but it did give her a seventh-place finish in the event. She also finished thirteenth in the all-around.

The best thing about the Worlds for Kristen was not her scores or her standing; it was the learning experience provided by the event, a key stepping-stone in her international career. "I learned that you have to stay focused," she said later. "You can't be distracted by things you can't control, like the draw or the judges' score. You just have to go out, keep going, and do the best you can. I think it helped me a lot with my confidence and how I handle myself at meets and with the pressure. I learned how to think for myself more and how to calm myself down."

Kristen had unveiled some brand-new moves in her uneven bars routines during the Worlds. After the competition, she received one of the sport's ultimate honors. The code of points for gymnastics was rewritten in 1997, and in the new version was a move listed as the "Maloney," which can be seen on a video on Kristen's Web site. "I was surprised and excited. I was kind of like in shock," she said after hearing the news.

Kristen came into the 1998 American Classic competition in Orlando, Florida, ready to defend her title, which she did in short order. She won two golds, on beam and floor exercises, and in the all-around, she outscored Olympian Dominique Dawes, three-time national champ Kim Zmeskal, and 1997 national co-champion Kristy Powell.

A month after her classes ended at Pen Argyl High School, Kristen headed off to Canada to take part in the Senior Pacific Alliance Championships, a meet that pitted ten national teams against each other. Prior to the event, Kristen had been experiencing a lot of soreness in her shin. It turned out to be a small stress fracture in the tibia. But she ignored the pain and gave an inspired performance, leading the team to the gold medal and winning the all-around, too.

The Pacific Alliance event was, and still is, one of Kristen's favorite meets, more for its team spirit than for the medals she won. "It was just so much fun," she remembered. "The team came together so well, and we were such great friends. We just had a really great time and everything went so well."

July's Goodwill Games in New York continued Kristen's gold rush. Cheered on by hometown fans who'd driven three hours from Pennsylvania, Kristen was the last to do her beam routine. Ukraine's Olga Teslenko had scored a 9.725, and the next two finishers both scored 9.7 or higher, so Kristen would have to be near perfect to win.

"It's really nerve-racking, especially when everyone hit so well in the beginning," Kristen admitted later. "I just tried to stay calm and focused and tried not to worry about what the others did."

She performed a beautiful routine on the beam, but when she came off the beam, she was sure she had missed her chance to take the gold. She was convinced her routine wasn't her best. But when the judges awarded her a 9.775, she was happily surprised. She had won the gold medal. With that performance, many people began to consider Kristen one of America's best young gymnasts.

"It's weird to hear people refer to me as one of the top gymnasts in the country or things like that," the seventeen-year-old champion said modestly. "I'll see my routine on TV and I'll be, like, 'Wow.' I have a hard time believing that's me on TV."

The 1998 U.S. Gymnastics Championships proved that Kristen was the steadiest gymnast on the women's team. Vanessa Atler had dazzled the crowd with scores of 9.850 in floor exercise and scores that topped 9.6 in both vault and beam, but her fall off the bars put her behind early in the all-around competition. Kristen, on the other hand, had consistently good scores, none of them lower than 9.387, and she won the title by almost a full point.

"I'm really excited and I'm kind of speechless right now," she said after winning the gold medal. "I don't know what to say or think. I'm so happy. I didn't really think about beating anyone. I just thought about going out there and doing my best.

"It was like a dream, like I actually didn't go through it," Kristen explained. "It was weird. I trained so hard for so long, I could finally say that it all paid off. I was so stunned that I didn't know what to think or what to say."

Kristen capped the year by being named one of eleven finalists for the Sullivan Award, an honor given each year to the country's top amateur athlete. At seventeen, she was the youngest of all the finalists. She also was voted the U.S. Female Athlete of the Year by her fellow athletes, and Gymnast of the Year by USA Gymnastics.

In March 1999, Kristen led the American team to a silver medal at the International Team Championships in Richmond, Virginia. Finishing second in the all-around, just .688 points behind Romania's Simona Amanar, Kristen was the only American to finish in the top five. She had the best score on vault as well.

In the spring of 1999, Kristen graduated from Pen Argyl High School. Because of her popularity, she was nominated for another honor— prom queen! She also won and accepted a scholarship to UCLA.

The stress fracture in her shin bothered Kristen all spring, and she was forced to curtail her training and cut back on competitions. At the 1999 Nationals, her leg was heavily taped, and landings, especially in the vault, were quite painful. Still, she was looking forward to the event, especially seeing her friends and fellow gymnasts. "That's what I was looking forward to most," she said. "I was real excited to see everyone. I've been out with an injury, so I haven't seen a lot of my friends in months. Defending my title is just icing on the cake."

Holding on to her title would definitely not be easy with the pain in her shin. "It was pretty sore at this morning's workout," she said prior to the meet. "But I try not to think about it. With the adrenaline running, I can push [the pain] to the back of my mind."

Unlike the 1998 Nationals, where Vanessa Atler's fall on uneven bars came in the preliminaries, the winner of the 1999 championships would be decided in the final rotation. Fifteen seconds into Vanessa's bars routine, she lost her grip on the Comaneci salto once again, allowing Kristen to take a decisive lead and win the all-around. Kristen became the first woman gymnast to win back-to-back titles since Kim Zmeskal won three straight from 1990 to 1992.

In the Event Finals, Kristen competed only in two events, and her sore shin forced her to cut short her bars routine after she lost her grip and fell. With the Worlds less than two months away, Kristen and her coach decided not to risk further injury by competing in other events.

The World Championships were the most important event of the year, and even Kristen felt the pressure. "I get so nervous, I just freak," she said before the meet.

While the American team's sixth-place results

in Tianjin were a letdown, Kristen provided several highlights, including a 9.550 score on the balance beam and a 9.662 on the floor, despite her music stopping midway through her routine. She was happy with her performance, although she thought the judges had underrated her performance on the beam. But on the whole "my routines were solid," she said. "As long as you do your best, you should be happy. And I know I did."

On October 14, at the height of the competition in Tianjin, Kristen fell off the bars during a practice routine. When she got to her feet, she felt a sharp pain in her knee. It turned out to be a torn ligament. The mishap forced Kristen to miss the Event Finals, but there was also a positive side to the injury. It was a wake-up call for Kristen. She had competed in pain for more than a year. She now had to face the fact that she would finally have to have surgery after the Worlds ended. "I guess everything happens for a reason," she wrote in her on-line diary. "I guess my body needed a break."

Despite her problems, the Worlds were a great adventure for the team, and for Kristen especially. She shared a hotel room with teammates Elise Ray and Vanessa Atler and enjoyed seeing the sights and shopping. Everything was so cheap that she couldn't resist buying shoes, shirts, jeans, and all kinds of small gifts for friends and family.

Reading gymnastics reports from 1998 and 1999, one might think that Kristen and Vanessa Atler were fierce rivals, but the pair are actually very good friends. "It's a friendly rivalry," Kristen explained. "We compete for the U.S.A., for our country, and not against each other."

In her spare time, Kristen enjoys listening to music ranging from country to R&B to dance music. A movie fan as well, she likes films starring Tom Cruise. She loves animals and has a dog named Silkie and two cats, Fluffy and Diddy.

Kristen underwent surgery on her leg and knee in the fall of 1999, and it was a success. She spent most of the end-of-the-year holidays recuperating. She found herself in an unusual position, either lying down or on crutches. Her fans flooded her with get-well cards, and she was grateful for the support and good wishes. Her shin was feeling better, too, with less pain than she had felt in years.

While she had to sit out the beginning of the 2000 season, she still has her sights set on Sydney. Despite the Americans' showing in Tianjin, Kristen remains optimistic about the team's Olympics hopes. "We have great potential for placing next year," she wrote in her on-line diary. "We didn't have Jennie [Thompson] or Alyssa [Beckerman] because of injuries, plus me and Ness [Atler] were both hurting. We were definitely not at 100 percent. So they're going to be surprised when we come in there next year and kick some butt."

Kristen has several goals if she makes it to Sydney. The first is for the U.S. team to finish in the top three. Then she hopes to make the all-around finals and finish in the top five. She also hopes to make the Event Finals in beam and floor exercise, her favorite event.

"The Olympics are the ultimate goal in gymnastics, but it's not the ultimate goal in life," Kristen says. "If people don't know me in ten years, I don't care, as long as I've been successful in what I'm doing. I just want to go to college and be happy."

COMPETITION HIGHLIGHTS

1999 World Championships, 6th team

1999 U.S. Gymnastics Championships, 1st AA, 6th UB, 2nd BB

1999 International Team Championships, 2nd team, 2nd AA, 1st V

1998 U.S. Gymnastics Championships, 1st AA, 2nd BB, 4th UB, VT, and FX

1998 Goodwill Games, 1st BB

1998 Pacific Alliance Championships, 1st team and
      AA, 3rd BB(tie), 4th UB

1998 American Classic, 1st AA, BB, and FX, 8th VT

1998 Visa American Cup, 3rd AA, 4th BB, 5th VT, UB,
      and FX

1997 World Gymnastics Championships, 6th team,
      14th AA, 7th BB

1997 U.S. Gymnastics Championships, 4th AA, 2nd VT,
      5th BB, 3rd FX

1997 American Classic, 1st AA

Vanessa Atler

No one should be fooled by Vanessa Atler's so-called uneven bars jinx. While her falls have received plenty of media attention, Nessa, as she is known to friends and fans, is one of America's brightest Olympic hopes. Combining strength, speed, power, and impressive acrobatic ability, Vanessa is capable of performing difficult moves with a spectacular style and skill that can often translate into high scores. A pretty young woman with a winning smile, she also has the spark and personality to transcend the limits of her sport, just like Mary Lou Retton and Nadia Comaneci, to whom Vanessa has been compared.

Bela Karolyi, who coached both Mary Lou and Nadia, noted, "In many ways, they are very similar. I would say that Vanessa is one of the biggest talents we've had in many years. Her physical abilities match the better gymnasts I have coached." As Nadia Comaneci herself put it, "She has it all."

Along with Kristen Maloney, Vanessa is regarded as one of America's best woman gymnasts. She is the team's best in vault. She's known for performing vaults—such as her front handspring, front layout, with a one and a half twist—that are complex and have extremely high levels of difficulty. When she does this vault, she propels herself five feet above the vaulting horse and then spins in the air one and a half times before landing. Vanessa may be the only woman gymnast to do that successfully in competition. She's also one of the few women to score a perfect 10 in vault under new scoring rules that went into effect in 1997. Her strong tumbling skills and fluid dance skills have made floor exercise another strong point in her performances.

At the 1997 National Championships, one of Vanessa's vaults amazed even TV commentator and former Olympian Michelle Dussere-Farrell. "That vault was so difficult," she told viewers, "that I can't even begin to explain how difficult it is."

Vanessa is also a fearless competitor, unafraid to try new and challenging moves. "I'd have to say I'm lucky I'm not afraid of throwing scary tricks," Vanessa observed. "I really look forward to trying out new skills."

But what really makes Vanessa unique is the combination of her explosive power, her athleticism, and her great speed, especially as she races down the runway toward the springboard and vault. She's been clocked on the runway at a speed of nearly 18 miles per hour, one mile an hour faster than her closest competitors. Vanessa's been measured hitting the vaulting springboard with an impact close to 2,000 pounds. (That same speed and power, however, can result in missed grips on the bars and work against her there.)

Vanessa Marie Atler was born in Valencia, California, on February 17, 1982. Her first ambition was to be a cheerleader, but she soon joined the thousands of young girls who were inspired to take up gymnastics by Mary Lou Retton. As a toddler, Vanessa was tiny. Her size led her parents—Nanette, a tennis teacher, and Ted, an electronics technician—to decide not to teach her tennis. Ice-skating and gymnastics seemed better choices, but the family couldn't afford ice skates, so she was enrolled in gymnastics classes, which she took to immediately. She quickly forgot about being a cheerleader. Vanessa was so eager, her mother recalls, that she would put her leotard on hours before it was time to go to class. Someday, Vanessa believed, she would be famous.

"I fell totally in love with gymnastics," Vanessa remembered. "I became more involved as I went along." She joined a local gym in Palmdale where she met and became good friends with Jamie Dantzscher. In 1990 at the age of eight, she entered her first meet, the Balloon Classic, and she finished with the highest scores of any competitor, beating even the older girls. Training more than thirty hours a week, Vanessa quickly moved from a level 5 gymnast to the top category, Elite, in four years.

But when eleven-year-old Vanessa finished last in her first meet as an Elite gymnast, her parents decided she needed better training and coaching. So in early 1994 she joined the Charter Oak Gliders in Covina, California, under the guidance of coaches Beth and Steve Rybacki. The next year Vanessa entered her first national meet, the U.S. Classic. She placed first in beam and vault, second in floor exercises, and third in the junior all-around.

Vanessa's dedication to her sport was so strong that not even the earthquake that shook California in 1994 could prevent her from getting to the gym. "My whole family had to sleep in a tent in the backyard for a while, and because the freeways were closed, it took two hours to get to the gym," Vanessa recalled. "Rain or earthquakes, we still have practice."

In 1995 she made the U.S. National Team. A year later she won the junior division all-around at the American Classic. If the optional scores had been added in, Vanessa would have finished higher than all but two senior-level competitors, including several members of the Magnificent Seven. Her total score was nearly a whole point ahead of her closest competitor.

Later that year she won the 1996 junior all-around gold medal and was crowned the new junior national champion. She also captured a gold medal in floor exercise.

Following the Atlanta Olympics, Vanessa entered her first senior event, the U.S. vs. the World competition, a professional event in which she served as a substitute for Olympian Shannon Miller. She was the only non-Olympian to make the team.

Vanessa's scores at the 1996 Nationals were good enough to qualify her to compete for a place on the Olympic team, but that was not to be. International gymnastics rules stated that female gymnasts had to be at least fifteen during the calendar year of the Olympics. Because she would not be fifteen until February 1997, Vanessa ended up watching the 1996 Olympics at home.

The 1997 Visa American Cup competition drew a top-ranked group of international gymnasts, including twenty-two Olympians who had competed in Atlanta. The event was a showcase for both established Olympic-level gymnasts and up-and-coming competitors. Vanessa, Kristen Maloney, Shannon Miller, and Amy Chow were just a few of the gymnasts who were there. Vanessa, now fifteen, gave an impressive performance, even though she was facing more experienced competitors. She won two Event Finals, taking the gold medal in beam and vault.

She continued her winning ways and, at the 1997 Nationals, was at her best for most of the meet. But Vanessa was nervous, as she would later admit. She took the gold medal in the vault and tied for fifth in floor exercise. After her first routine on uneven bars, she received a score of 9.325. If she did as well on her second one, it seemed certain she would take sole possession of the all-around gold.

Kristy Powell, Vanessa's closest competitor, had scored a 9.3 in her final beam routine, putting more pressure on Vanessa. As Vanessa prepared for her final bars routine, she couldn't help looking at the scoreboard to see Powell's scores.

"I was nervous on bars because I looked at the scoreboard," Vanessa said later. "My coaches [Steve and Beth Rybacki] keep telling me not to do that, but I couldn't help it."

Vanessa was also nervous because she was trying a new move—a Comaneci salto—on the bars that she had never done before in competition.

Perhaps as a result of her nervousness, Vanessa lost her grip during her final bars routine and fell. She was forced to restart her routine. Her 8.650 score still was good enough to capture the title of national champion, but it allowed Kristy Powell to tie her, and the pair ended up sharing the honor. A first-place finish would normally have qualified her for a place on the 1997 World Championship team. But again, Vanessa fell short of the age requirement: all Worlds competitors had to be sixteen by the end of that year, and Vanessa was just forty-eight days shy of the deadline, a heartbreaking twist of fate for her and her family. She ended up heading home while Kristy Powell packed her bags for a trip to Switzerland.

"I was pleased with how I did," Vanessa said, summing up her overall performance. "I just wanted to come here and do my stuff and not worry about where I finished." Vanessa was somewhat philosophical about the new age rule. "I wanted to come in, do my new tricks and have fun," she said. "I was disappointed at first, but I can't do anything about it. I think it's a fair rule. It's good in some cases and it's bad in some cases, but it's definitely bad for me."

But the 1997 Nationals were noteworthy for Vanessa, nonetheless. She had made the jump from junior national champion to senior champion in a single year. She was only the sixth American gymnast, and the first since Dominique Moceanu, to do so.

Vanessa struck gold twice at the July 1998 Pacific Alliance Championships, a test event for the more important Pan Am Games to be held the following summer. She easily topped the competition in the vault and the floor exercise, winning gold in both events. The event also provided Vanessa with tremendous momentum for the upcoming Goodwill Games. "I felt I could place high in both events," Vanessa commented, "but I wasn't quite sure. This is a good way to go into the Goodwill Games. I know the competition here isn't as strong as what will be in New York, but this is a great confidence builder for me."

Vanessa's confidence was justified. She won gold medals in floor exercise and vault at the Goodwill Games, but despite her victory, her reaction was subdued. Standing on a chair so she could be seen, Vanessa told a cluster of reporters, "My performance on a 1 to 10 scale was maybe an 8. It was not spectacular. I did well and I was proud of myself, but I still felt there was room for improvement."

She was being modest. Her gold medal in vault—Vanessa's favorite event—was the first time an American had taken the gold on the vault at the Goodwill Games. Vanessa would always consider this competition one of her most memorable gymnastics experiences.

The 1998 Nationals, however, were tough for Vanessa. She was named national champion in floor exercise, and she took a silver in the vault, but she again fell off the uneven bars. The mistake cost her the title, and she finished second in the all-around behind Kristen Maloney. Even though she scored a 9.8 in her final bars routine, her two falls off the bars in the preliminaries made the difference between first and second place in the all-around.

Vanessa ended her 1998 season on a high note at the Australia Cup meet in Melbourne. She won gold medals in the all-around, vault, and floor exercise, triumphing over three of Australia's best gymnasts: Zeena McLaughlin, Allana Slater, and Trudy McIntosh, and China's Fan Wen.

Vanessa appeared to be on a roll as 1999 began. Just days shy of her seventeenth birthday, she easily dominated the American Classic meet in February, finishing with top scores in all four events. She handily defeated her closest competitor, Jennie Thompson, by more than 1.5 points. But there was trouble on the horizon.

In March Vanessa participated in the French Telecom International meet in Paris. She finished second in the all-around, right behind defending world champion Svetlana Khorkina. In the Event Finals, she won vault, then scored a 9.825. It was the highest score of the entire meet. But in the final round on the floor, Vanessa fell and sprained her ankle. Although she was quick to say the injury was not serious, her ankle would bother her for the rest of the year.

Prior to the 1999 U.S. Gymnastics Championships, *USA Today* published a feature article about Vanessa. The newspaper praised her skills, saying she could easily follow in the footsteps of Nadia Comaneci and Mary Lou Retton. She had, the reporter noted, "the spunk, sparkle, and skill to fill those big shoes." Nadia herself was quoted in the article, agreeing with the description.

Vanessa's coach, Beth Rybacki, however, warned that it was premature to be making such comparisons. "There's still a lot of work to do before the Olympics," she cautioned.

Vanessa was looking forward to the Nationals, not only because that meet would provide a rematch with Kristen Maloney but also because the "Showdown in Sacramento" would be in her home state, and her family and friends would be there to watch her. "I'm already excited," she said before the competition began. "I'm glad it's in California. All my family will be there. I feel so alone when I'm by myself on the road."

At the 1999 Nationals, Vanessa led the all-around till the final rotation. A mistake-free bars routine would have clinched the title, but Vanessa again grew nervous and distracted and fell. Her 9.175 dropped her into second place and gave Kristen Maloney the all-around gold.

Two days later in the Event Finals, Vanessa redeemed herself with gold medal performances on both vault and beam, and those two first-place finishes made her fall off the bars easier to take. "Tonight made me feel a lot better about myself," she said after finishing. "I feel really good going into Worlds. It's very exciting."

She did concede that her bars falls had shaken her confidence. "It's definitely mental," she admitted. "My workouts have been fine. I've talked to psychologists; thousands of people have tried to help me."

Despite losing the all-around, Vanessa remained friends with Kristen Maloney. "It's a rivalry," Vanessa explained, "but a friendly one. When I see her competing, I don't see her as a person. I think of her as an opponent. But off the floor, she's a good friend." With the 1999 World Championships approaching, Vanessa declared, "From here on in, we're on the same team. I'm looking forward to that."

Vanessa was eager to compete in her first World Championships meet, and she was also looking forward to competing as a member of a team. "We're like the best of friends," she said, describing the team's spirit. "We get along, and we know each other so well. We laugh constantly. We like to have fun, and I think we're a great team."

In the preliminary round of the team competition, Vanessa's mastery in floor exercise earned a 9.762 score but, more important, it clinched the Americans' place in the team finals.

Vanessa was quick to give credit to her teammates. "I think we did really great as a team," she commented after the prelims. "We were nervous about making the top six, and we know we can go out there and win a medal. The Worlds," she added, "doesn't make me nervous. It gets me pumped up. I think next time—the next competition—I'm going to go out and do a lot better. I think we got all our jitters out today."

Unfortunately—perhaps because of the loud Chinese crowd and her sore ankle—Vanessa lost her concentration and fell off the beam twice in the team finals. The falls were not the only reason for the American women's sixth-place finish, but they were nonetheless upsetting to Vanessa.

"It was the most nervous I have been in my entire life," she admitted later. "I don't know what happened. The crowd was really loud and that was hard. Most of us have never been to a World Championship before and [had to] deal with some of this stuff. It is hard not to concentrate on all of that. I think it was really tough for all of us, and I know it was hard for me."

On the positive side, Vanessa added, "I guess it's a good learning experience for next time, for the Olympics. You've just got to learn from it and not be so nervous next time."

The 1999 Worlds had been quite different from most of Vanessa's previous meets. "It's different than American or even regular international competition. It's such an important meet, and people are so intense about it. You can feel it, the tension. There's nothing you can really do about it, except try to be more mentally prepared."

By the summer of 1999, Vanessa was feeling the need to make changes not only in her routines and training but also in her coaches. After six years with Beth and Steve Rybacki, she announced she would be leaving the Charter Oak gym. The changes, she said, had nothing to do with her falls at the Nationals and Worlds.

Vanessa also had her injured ankle examined by a doctor. It turned out that Vanessa had a large bone chip. The doctor took one look at the X-rays and said, "Ouch! How did you compete on this?" He recommended she have surgery soon. Despite the bad news, Vanessa was relieved to learn that no serious damage had occurred as a result of competing on the ankle.

Vanessa later admitted that there were times in 1999 when she thought about quitting gymnastics. But her family constantly reminded her that she had worked hard, that she was talented, and that her best performances lay ahead of her.

Vanessa and her mother, Nanette, visited different gyms, met with several coaches, and eventually decided on Valeri Liukin, a former Olympic champion who was now running the

World Olympic Gymnastic Academy in Texas. Liukin had no doubts about Vanessa's abilities. "I think Vanessa is basically the best gymnast in America," he declared. "I'm going to try to calm her down and bring her confidence back."

In early November, Vanessa and Nanette moved from their home in California to an apartment in Plano, Texas. It was then announced that Bela Karolyi and his wife, Martha, would also be helping Vanessa come up with a new training schedule and regimen.

Vanessa visited the gym and met several of the World Academy gymnasts. At first she was nervous about whether the other girls would accept her, but she soon felt at ease and comfortable with them. That night, Vanessa, her mother, Bela, and Valeri had a long talk about Vanessa's career and training. Karolyi and Liukin were both highly enthusiastic about working with Vanessa, and their excitement was contagious. Suddenly Vanessa felt a renewed sense of pride and purpose.

Vanessa slowly got back into her training. The first day, after practice, Vanessa's ankle was sore and every muscle in her body felt tired. After all, she had not trained or worked out for more than a month. Massage therapy helped, and within three days, for the first time in weeks, Vanessa felt satisfied that her career was back on track. She realized her family had been right: she had worked too hard to give up the sport she loved and in which she excelled.

At the end of November, Vanessa had the bone chip surgically removed from her ankle. The doctor told her it was the biggest bone chip he had ever seen, even after years of working with football and hockey players from the Dallas Cowboys and the Dallas Stars. Vanessa, with her usual humor, joked, "See, that makes me tougher than all those football players."

Despite being sidelined, she was glad that her ankle had been taken care of and that some of the pressure she had been facing had eased. When Vanessa flew back to California for the Christmas holidays, she was happier than she had been in a long time. Vanessa shared those feelings with her fans in her on-line diary. That openness and her outgoing personality have endeared her to her fans, and she is not afraid to show her feelings in competition. "When I'm happy, I smile," she said simply. "When I fall, I get sad and cry. I'm very emotional."

Traveling overseas to international meets is something Vanessa loves, and she especially enjoys the challenge of competing against the world's best. "I've made a lot of friends at international competitions," she said. "Exchanging gifts with other gymnasts is fun. As for my gymnastics, when I see Russian, Romanian, and Chinese gymnasts, it makes me want to hurry home to start working on my gymnastics again."

At home, Vanessa is a somewhat private person. Although she likes meeting her fans, she is, according to her mother, fairly shy. She spends her spare time surfing sports-related Web sites on the Internet, watching *Seinfeld* and *I Love Lucy* reruns, and reading books like *Chicken Soup for the Teenage Soul*. She enjoys writing entries for her Web site and keeping a journal, which she may someday turn into a book. She also enjoys music, especially the songs of the Dixie Chicks, Mariah Carey, Jewel, and others. Her hobbies include cooking, shopping, and collecting things with butterfly themes. Vanessa loves dogs and has a golden retriever named George after George Costanza on *Seinfeld*. Someday, she says, she might like to be a sports psychologist.

The people Vanessa admires most are gymnasts like Dominique Dawes, Jaycie Phelps, and Kristen Maloney. She and fellow Californian Jamie Dantzscher are the closest of friends.

Vanessa's many admirers include not just fans but also gymnastics professionals who have worked with her and watched her. Those in the gymnastics community respect her for her dedication, style, and spirit as well as for her talent. "Vanessa's class is that of a true champion," says Elfi Schleigel, a champion Canadian gymnast turned NBC-TV commentator. Her longtime coach Steve Rybacki says simply, "She is a great person."

Vanessa realizes that Sydney may be her only shot at an Olympic medal and that her age might work against her, as it has in the past. "I'll be eighteen when I get to the Olympics, competing against sixteen-year-olds. Usually you're at your peak around sixteen. This is going to be my only shot.

"I think about it all the time," she added. Vanessa can keep those thoughts in perspective, however. "I want to have a great life, and my happiness isn't about whether or not I'm in the Olympics. But it would be the perfect ending."

COMPETITION HIGHLIGHTS

1999 World Championships, 6th team

1999 U.S. Gymnastics Championships, 2nd AA,
      1st V and BB

1999 American Classic/Pan Am Trials, 1st AA

1999   Paris Bercy, 2nd AA, 1st V

1999   Visa American Cup, 3rd AA, 1st BB and FX

1998   Australia Cup, 1st AA, V, and FX

1998   Goodwill Games, 1st V, 1st FX

1998   U.S. Gymnastics Championships, 2nd AA, V,
       1st FX

1997   U.S Gymnastics Championships, 1st AA, shared
       title with Kristy Powell

AMERICAN GYMNASTS CLOSE-UPS:
Elise Ray

As one reader of *International Gymnast* put it, Elise Ray is "the total package." Combining great form with the style, elegance, and grace of a dancer, Elise is a poised, pretty, and precise gymnast who makes difficult moves look easy. Her showing at the 1999 World Team Trials and the Tianjin World Championships demonstrated that she was a world-class athlete and a strong contender for a place on the 2000 Olympic team. Until recently Elise did not attract as much attention as some of her teammates did, but her rise up the ranks has been steady, and her best performances may be yet to come.

She's been a member of the national team since 1996 and for many years was considered a specialist on the uneven bars. In recent years, however, she has developed her skills in other events, especially floor exercise, where her flowing and expressive moves have earned high marks.

Off the floor, she is a typical giggly teenager who is admired and well liked by her friends and teammates because of her cheerfulness and caring nature. Her coach, Kelli Hill, once paid Elise the highest compliment a teenager could hope for: "If you were going through high school again, you'd want her as your best friend."

Mary Elise Ray was born on February 6, 1982, in Tallahassee, Florida, and grew up in Columbia, Maryland. Her father, Bill, is a psychotherapist, and her mother, Ellen, is a nurse-midwife. Elise took up gymnastics at age six at a local gym. "It started out as a class thing," Elise recalled. "I started in a recreation class. I think it was a tumbling class. I loved it so much, the coaches said I should join an actual gymnastics club. I just kept plugging away. I never tried any other sports, even when I was younger," Elise remembered. "I guess my biggest thing was being a Daisy, a younger version of a Girl Scout."

Elise advanced rapidly and soon found a more advanced gym. Her current coach, Kelli Hill, ran Hill's Gymnastics "right down the street," as Elise puts it, and she was happy to find a good gym so close to home. "I don't think I could ever live away from home," she has said.

Joining Hill's Angels was a turning point for Elise. Under Kelli Hill's guidance, Elise's talent blossomed, and she began to think that perhaps she might someday become a top-ranked gymnast. "There wasn't any specific time when I knew I could be a great gymnast," Elise said, "but Kelli had a great influence on me, helping me believe in myself and believe I could succeed. She really motivated me." At the time, Elise looked no further than her own gym to find heroes and role models. "My heroes when I started were probably the older girls in my gym," she said. "I really looked up to them. They were leaders to me."

Elise quickly rose to Elite status, the highest competitive level in the sport. "The pressure and intensity increased . . . but I was having fun, so I didn't worry too much about that," she recalled.

In 1994 at the U.S. Classic, Elise scored her first national success as an Elite gymnast when she won a silver medal on uneven bars and finished sixth in the junior all-around. She picked up a gold medal on balance beam at the 1996 U.S. Classic, which was quite gratifying for Elise. "I was most proud of my beam routine because it's a hard event to do," she said.

That year she also competed at her first National Championships and won an all-around bronze medal in the junior division.

Like her teammates, Elise watched the

Magnificent Seven's triumph on television. "I watched the games with my family at home," she recalled, "and I remember being so inspired and so excited for all the girls on the team."

In February 1997, Elise took part in the International Team Championships, a three-way meet between American, Chinese, and Romanian junior national teams. Elise won the silver medal in floor exercise and helped her team score a decisive victory. "I'm so excited," she said afterward. "It was such a fun meet. I wasn't expecting the United States to do so well, but we just went out and hit our routines."

By 1997, Vanessa Atler had graduated to the senior level, so Elise was one of the favorites to win a medal in the all-around at the 1997 Junior U.S. Championships. She was relaxed on the first day of the preliminaries and was leading the all-around competition after the first half. But on the second day she got nervous and slipped off the bars. The fall dropped her into fourth place and out of medal contention. In the Event Finals, Elise returned to her usual form and won the uneven bars competition, becoming the junior champion in the event. With her characteristically cheerful outlook, Elise said, "I'm happy with how I did."

The year 1998 marked her first season of competition as a senior. Elise quickly built up momentum as she gave impressive performances at a series of international events. In quick succession, she took silver medals in bars at the Pacific Alliance Championships, the Goodwill Games, and the Sagit Cup competition, a dual meet against Canada. The Goodwill Games medal was particularly noteworthy as Elise scored a 9.7 on bars. Only Svetlana Khorkina, the defending world and Olympic champion, scored higher.

Later in the year, she traveled to Tianjin, China, for the first time to participate in the China Cup tournament. Facing tough competition from a powerful Chinese team, she won a bronze on beam and silver in floor exercises. Her ninth-place finish in the all-around was the highest score of any American at the event. In fact, she was the top foreign finisher of all.

Elise capped the year with a gold medal performance on the bars at the 1998 U.S. Gymnastics Championships. The event marked a major step up for sixteen-year-old Elise. The former junior bars champion was now senior bars champ, and Elise was suddenly being viewed as a possible Olympic candidate for 2000.

She was briefly sidelined in 1999 with a pulled back muscle that kept her out of the Pan Am Games. In spite of her many recent successes, Elise, like any competitive athlete, experienced some moments of doubt about her abilities and career around this time. "I was doubting myself and my gymnastics so much that I felt like I didn't want to continue," she observed. "It was such a terrible feeling, but I think I had to go through that in order to get stronger."

Elise quickly regained her optimism and continued her winning ways. At the International Team Championships in Richmond, Virginia, she scored a 9.80 on bars, the highest score of any at the meet. Her efforts played a key role in helping the United States win the silver medal. At the Canada Dual meet in May, she took first place in floor exercise, second in beam, and third in the vault. Although Elise had been known as a bars specialist until then, this meet served notice that she was more than a one-event wonder. She showed how much her skills had grown by performing a new and difficult move on vault (laid out Yurchenko with a one-and-a-half twist), and she unveiled a new floor exercise routine set to the Spanish rhythm of "Malaguena," which not only won the event but won Elise many new fans. "I was really looking forward to doing floor, so it was great to win the gold," Elise said. "The pressure [of the all-around] was off, and I just had fun out there."

Elise, like Kristen Maloney, enjoys team competitions most. "I love team competition because it's like everyone working together," she said in mid-1999. "We have a great team this year, and I look forward to learning more about everyone on it. I don't really know what to expect yet, but I'm really excited."

The excitement continued in August 1999 at the U.S. Classic event, the final qualifier for the upcoming U.S. Gymnastics Championships. Elise scored higher than 9.7 on all events except vault, and won two of the four events she entered (bars and floor). At the Nationals, she again demonstrated her growing floor exercise skills as she took the gold with a stunning performance that received a 9.775 score. She would have finished higher in the all-around, but a slip on the uneven bars dropped her into sixth place.

Elise's training had been going well, which bolstered her confidence as the World Team Trials approached. "I've been having really good practices," she said. "My spirits have really been up, and I've been excited to compete, which helps. I've been trying to really work on positive thinking, and mental as well as physical training.

"I'm so excited to be here for the first time," she said prior to the meet. "I have been training so hard," she added. "Everything I have worked for comes down to this year. My goal is to make the World Team."

Elise began the all-around on her best event, uneven bars. She displayed such great form that one writer said her legs appeared to be "super-glued" together. Her score, 9.772, would have been even higher had it not been for a small hop on her dismount. Her vault was a solid 9.256, and her precise beam routine won a 9.537. While she had a misstep or two in her floor exercise, she still earned a 9.625 score. She was the top qualifier for the Worlds team, and her 76.378 score was nearly a point ahead of the scores of her nearest competitors, Jeanette Antolin and Alyssa Beckerman.

The World Team Trials put Elise in the spotlight and served notice that she was one of America's best gymnasts. Her performance had been clean, consistent, and exciting to watch. Elise, in the words of the *Kansas City Star*, "could have filled an entire highlight reel herself."

Elise could hardly wait for the Worlds. "I've never been to the World Championships before," she said, "so that motivates me. The thing I'm looking forward to most about the Worlds is being with a team and working together toward a common goal." Always a down-to-earth person, Elise reminded reporters that she would soon be back at home, making up the homework she had missed.

Tianjin marked Elise's first Worlds, although it was not her first trip to China. "It really helped me, having been to China before and experiencing all the differences," she said. But she was still a bit unprepared for the raucous and rowdy Chinese fans. "They do get pretty excited," she said, laughing. "I didn't really know it would be quite like that. It was hard when I first heard all the noise, but then I just focused more and blocked it out. It was intense and nerve-racking but once I was competing, I felt very confident and prepared."

Elise's eighth-place showing in the all-around was a pleasant surprise for the U.S. team. She finished just .001 point behind seventh-place finisher Huang Mandan of China. In the Event Finals, Elise also shone, scoring a 9.662 on the floor, and her bars score of 9.637 put her in seventh place on that apparatus.

The Worlds competition was a thrilling experience for Elise. She regards her performance in Tianjin as one of her greatest moments. She also learned a lot from the meet. "Now that I have this under my belt, I

KRISTEN MALONEY

MORGAN
WHITE

VANESSA ATLER

JENNIE
THOMPSON

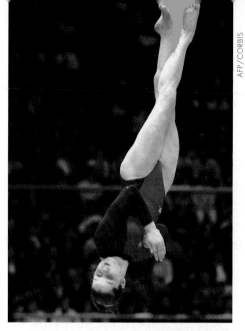

ELISE RAY

JAMIE DANTZSCHER

ALYSSA
BECKERMAN

JEANETTE
ANTOLIN

DOMINIQUE
MOCEANU

AMY CHOW

know what to expect, which will definitely help in the future," she said.

Elise believes the competition is good preparation for the Olympics. "I think the pressures will be in a way similar but more intense," she explained. "I feel like I have a taste of what it will be like next year, which is good because I can prepare myself even more.

Her coach, Kelli Hill, agreed. "I think this was a great opportunity for Elise. In our country she's kind of overshadowed. She's not the powerhouse gymnast that the United States is used to, but some people compare her to [Svetlana] Khorkina. I think she's actually a gymnast of her own. Elise is all about elegance."

In addition to elegance, Elise is known for her beautiful lines, her great arm and leg extensions, her toe point, and her body alignment. She uses her hands and facial expression to add depth and graceful elements to her performances. Many observers have commented on Elise's ballet-like moves. Surprisingly, she has never taken formal ballet lessons, but she has worked with choreographers in the gym. Her mother was a dancer in college, so Elise credits her grace to good genes. "The dance elements," she said, "come really easy and naturally to me."

For good luck, her mother gave Elise an angel pin, which she wears on her warm-up suit. She has other good-luck charms such as a Cookie Monster beanie doll that was given to her by her friend, Magnificent Seven member Dominique Dawes. Dominique used to keep it nearby whenever she performed on uneven bars, and she's lent it to Elise to bring her luck. Needless to say, the charms seem to be working.

When she's not doing gymnastics, Elise enjoys watching movies, doing craft activities, shopping, or just being with her family. She often takes Friday nights off from gymnastics to do things with friends. Her hobbies include collecting picture frames, making scrapbooks and memory albums, and reading. Her favorite book is *The Divine Secrets of the Ya-Ya Sisterhood* by Rebecca Wells. She also enjoys listening to music. Like Vanessa Atler, Elise is a Dixie Chicks fan.

Elise has accepted a scholarship to the University of Michigan. She loves animals and plans to become a veterinarian. "I am really looking forward to that," Elise said.

As far as the Olympics Games are concerned, Elise only recently set her sights on Sydney. "I wasn't sure," she said, "and then I suddenly realized it's so close, and I thought, why not just go for it?"

Coach Kelli Hill thinks that relaxed attitude is just part of Elise's personality. "I don't think gymnastics is her whole life," Kelli explained. "I think she does gymnastics because she absolutely loves the sport."

Elise has clear objectives as far as her training for the Olympics is concerned. "My main goal right now is to get my start values on vault up, but in general I need to work on the little things, perfecting everything and making it 100 percent consistent," she noted. "My hopes for the Olympics are to bring home a medal for our country, whether it be team or individual, or both. Hopefully both!"

COMPETITION HIGHLIGHTS

2000   Aussie Haircare Invitationals, 1st AA, V, UB, and FX

1999   World Championships, 8th AA, 7th UB, 6th team

1999   World Team Trials, 1st AA

1999   U.S. Championships, 6th AA and V, 5th BB, 1st FX

1999   Canada Dual, 3rd V, 2nd UB, 1st FX

1998   China Cup, 3rd BB, 2nd FX

1998   Goodwill Games, 2nd UB

1998   U.S. Gymnastics Championships, 5th AA, 1st UB

AMERICAN GYMNASTS CLOSE-UPS:
Morgan White

There's an old saying: "When one door closes, another one usually opens." Morgan White's career bears that out. At the 1999 World Team Trials, Morgan finished just out of the running for the alternate spot on the Worlds team. But when alternate Alyssa Beckerman was diagnosed with a broken wrist a week later, Morgan moved up into her spot and won a trip to Tianjin. Then when Jennie Thompson hurt her ankle while training for the Worlds, Morgan moved up again, this time to a full-fledged competitor.

At the 1999 Pan Am Games, the site of Morgan's biggest triumph so far, she was again slated to be an alternate. But when Vanessa Atler had to withdraw because of a sprained ankle, Morgan seized the opportunity once more and won the all-around gold medal.

Morgan's good luck may have been the result of her teammates' bad breaks. But Morgan also has worked extremely hard to put herself in a position where she could benefit from those circumstances, proving the truth of another old saying: "If you work really hard, you can increase your chances of being lucky."

Early in her career, Morgan White's main goal in gymnastics was to do well enough at meets to see her name in the newspaper. She's certainly done that and more. Since winning the junior national championship in 1998, Morgan has proved to be a world-class competitor, and she has a host of medals to prove it. The youngest member of the Worlds team, Morgan provided gymnastics fans with some of 1999's most memorable moments.

A photograph taken at the 1999 Pan Am Games—where Morgan surprised many by taking the gold medal in the face of stiff competition from some of the world's best gymnasts—shows not only Morgan's style and grace but also her look of steely-eyed determination. In that meet, she followed in the footsteps of one of America's greatest gymnasts, Shannon Miller, who had won the event four years earlier. That meet marked Morgan's first major triumph as a senior gymnast and was a competitive coming-of-age for one of the sport's brightest new stars.

Morgan Lindsey White was born in West Bend, Wisconsin, on June 27, 1983. The third of three children, Morgan eventually moved with her family to Florida where she became a member of the American Twisters gym in Fort Lauderdale. Her mother, Debbie, is a teacher, and her father, Ron, is an account executive.

As a little girl, Morgan enjoyed watching gymnastics on TV. When she was five, Morgan recalled, "One of my neighbor's kids got a trampoline. I begged my mom for one, too. Instead we enrolled in a Mommy and Me tumbling class. I loved it. I've been doing gymnastics ever since."

Morgan was a quick learner, and she progressed rapidly. She stepped up her competition schedule and, by 1996, had made it to the Junior National Championships. Her first finish at a championship meet was twenty-third place in the all-around, but Morgan soon improved on that start, thanks to a new gym. Morgan had begun to feel the need to train with more advanced Elite gymnasts, so in 1997 she and her family moved to Fairfield, Ohio, to train with Mary Lee Tracy at the Cincinnati Gymnastics Academy, alongside Alyssa Beckerman and Jennie Thompson. Morgan now lives in Fairfield.

On her first day at the gym, Morgan was utterly awestruck. There, performing right in front of her was Kim Zmeskal, the 1991 world champion. "She's been my favorite gymnast since I was little," Morgan said. "I was scared going in, but once I started working out, I found that she's just like any other person."

Morgan took to her new gym and coach right away. She credits Mary Lee Tracy with boosting her skills and her confidence. Joining the Cincinnati Gymnastics Academy was a turning point in Morgan's life. She found that her new gym and coach made a difference in her attitude and outlook as well as in her gymnastics.

Morgan says that Mary Lee Tracy is a big inspiration to her. "She really made me believe in myself, and all the extra stuff she puts into her gymnasts—sports psychology, Bible study, trainers, all stuff I didn't have, that most gyms don't have—that's what makes the difference."

Results were quick in coming. At the 1997 American Classic in New Haven, Connecticut, Morgan finished fifth in the junior all-around. She made her international debut, too, when she visited Brussels, Belgium, for the International Artistic Gymnastics Challenge, where she won gold on bars and placed fourth in the all-around. Then she headed to South America for the Pan Am Championships in Medellín, Colombia. She captured a silver on bars and helped the junior team take second place.

Although she only finished twelfth in the all-around at the 1997 Junior Nationals, she

took home the gold medal in bars and finished
fourth in the all-around at that year's Artistic
Challenge meet.

Her gold medal run continued in 1998. At
the American Classic in Orlando, Florida, she
again captured the gold medal in the uneven
bars and finished fifth in the all-around. Her
showing at the U.S. Classic in San Antonio,
Texas, was even more impressive. She dominated the junior competition, coming home
with a silver in bars and floor, and gold medals
in the all-around and beam.

Continuing her Pan Am Games streak, Morgan took the gold medal on uneven bars at the
1998 Junior Pan American Gymnastics Championships. Her bars score of 9.587 was the
highest given out at the event. She added to
her collection of medals with a team gold and
two silvers—in all-around and beam.

Because of her spectacular finish at the U.S.
Classic, Morgan thought she had a shot at winning the junior all-around title at the upcoming
1998 U.S. Gymnastics Championships in Indianapolis. But she tried not to think about it too
much for fear that it might make her nervous.
Instead she concentrated on performing the
best she could and hitting all her events.

While most of the crowd in Market Square
Arena seemed focused on Vanessa Atler and

Kristen Maloney's battle for the senior all-around title, fans also got a glimpse of the future as Morgan, now fifteen, put on another dazzling display.

More than 5,000 fans—a larger-than-usual crowd for the junior competition—attended the event. "I've never competed in front of this many people," Morgan said later. "I wasn't expecting to see that many here. It was scary but fun. The cheers motivate you to do your best."

If Morgan was nervous, it didn't show, and the cheers also must have helped. She won the junior national title, took the gold in floor exercises, tied for first place in the uneven bars, and won a silver medal on beam. Morgan was ecstatic with her showing, but she knew she had another challenge—senior status—ahead of her.

"It was great, unexpected at first, and overwhelming," she said of the 1998 Nationals. "Now that I'm [in the] senior division I have to forget about it and start all over. I did gain a lot of confidence from it."

Morgan admitted being a little apprehensive about competing as a senior in 1999, especially when she realized her competition would be gymnasts like Vanessa Atler and Kristen Maloney. "It's the big time," she observed. The pressure was definitely more intense.

"I just try not to focus on it," Morgan stated. "I'm just going to go out there and do my normal gymnastics, no matter if I'm a junior or a senior. Hopefully, I can reach my goals and place where I want to place."

In April, Morgan was part of a six-woman team facing a talented Chinese team in the two-day China Dual meet. Morgan was excited about the event and thrilled to be on the same team as her hero, 1991 national champion Kim Zmeskal.

Morgan competed in all four events, scoring a 9.5 on floor and beam, and a 9.7 on bars. Late in the competition, the Chinese team took the lead, and Morgan's vault performance would make the difference between winning and losing. A 9.312 score would tie the score. Instead she got a 9.5, and the U.S. women edged out the Chinese 113.462 to 113.274.

Morgan celebrated her sixteenth birthday that summer by heading to a local amusement center in Cincinnati, playing games, and winning an armful of stuffed animals and other prizes. Morgan, who enjoys bike riding, also got a ten-speed bike, personalized stationery, clothes, and perfume for gifts.

She trained hard in preparation for the Pan Am Games, scheduled for July in Winnipeg, Canada. She would be the youngest member

of the senior American team and she admitted
to being a bit nervous. The Pan Am Games
would be just her third meet as a senior. "It's
really fun to be competing as a senior," she
said. "I was very nervous coming into Pan Am
Games because it is a big meet with gymnasts
I have never competed against, plus I am the
youngest."

Few expected Morgan to win at the Pan Am
Games, but her coach, Mary Lee Tracy, thought
she had a good chance. Before leaving for
Canada, Mary Lee told Morgan she was "consistent and a competitor. You have a chance to
win it. You can do it."

Her coach's confidence proved to be war-
ranted. Morgan's solid showing helped the
team take the silver medal, and she won a
bronze on bars. The biggest prize of all, however, came in the all-around.

Morgan did well in the all-around, and by
the final rotation, she knew she was in third
place. A solid routine on bars would give her a
lock on the bronze, but she did even better
than expected: she earned the gold medal. It
was a remarkable achievement for the sixteen-
year-old athlete.

After Morgan finished, Mary Lee dialed
Debbie and Ron White's home in Ohio, then
handed the cellular phone to Morgan. When

her parents heard the news, they were ecstatic.
Debbie screamed with delight, "I can't believe
it!" Her father, Ron, remained calm. "I knew
you could do it," he told his daughter.

Morgan got another thrill after the meet.
Shannon Miller, the most decorated gymnast
in U.S. history, was in the audience at the
meet. When asked about Morgan's win, she
told reporters, "She's one of those gymnasts
who come in silently, quietly. She's consistent
in workout and consistent in the meet. She
reminds me of me."

When Morgan heard what Shannon had
said, she was flabbergasted. "That's just like,
wow, too amazing!" she exclaimed. "I'm still in
shock, I guess."

When she regained her composure, Morgan
told the media, "I knew I would be a consistent competitor in the all-around. I thought I
could do well if I just believed in myself, but I
am still in shock that I won. This builds my
confidence enormously."

"Morgan did a great job," said coach Mary
Lee Tracy. "She has to concentrate on getting
some bigger skills and learning some new
things, but the biggest thing is she made a
statement in an international meet that she is
a contender and a competitor. Morgan proved
she could do it tonight." Tracy added, "This is

wonderful for her going into the National Championships next month."

The U.S. Gymnastics Championships meet "is very important to me," Morgan confirmed. "It's a qualifier for the Worlds and really good experience for the Olympics in 2000. I obviously would love to make it to Worlds, but I'm basically not focusing on rankings. I just want to do my routines like I do them in the gym. Then I'll be happy."

At the 1999 Nationals in Sacramento, California, Morgan won a silver medal in floor exercise and tied for third on bars, but her seventh place finish in the all-around was a letdown for her. She was dissatisfied with her scores, but her coach definitely was not. "Morgan did a great job," Mary Lee said. "She's a little disappointed because she's seventh and she was hoping to do better. But it was a good experience because she's young and she's going to get stronger. She's such a competitor, she wants everything perfect. She just has to be patient with herself. Right now she's where she should be."

Morgan was eagerly anticipating the World Team Trials in Kansas City, Missouri, not only to see if she could win a place on the Worlds team but also because her entire family, including her brothers Dustin and Dylan, would get to watch her. "I am really ready for this meet," she said. "I've been training really well, so I just need to go out there and compete like I have been training. I just want to hit my events both days and hopefully make the Worlds team."

At the trials, Morgan worked her way up to fourth place, then faltered on the floor and stepped out of bounds. She still scored a 9.387, but she finished out of the running for a place on the team.

The next two weeks were an emotional roller-coaster ride for Morgan. "It stunk not being able to originally make the team," she later explained. "I still remember after trials when I hadn't made it and how upset I was. I thought my season was over. Then I was excited about having an off-season and being able to learn a few skills, upgrade a bit, and get ready for the important 2000 season. Then all of a sudden I found out I was going, and it was like, 'Uh-oh,' but it's been such an experience. Just being able to experience a whole World Championships is so important."

When Morgan got to China, she found out she would be competing in place of Jennie Thompson. "Now I'm here competing, it's kind of strange," she observed. "It's really exciting. It's kind of hard when I found out I was going to be competing, because that meant Jennie was done and she wouldn't be competing. That's tough because she deserves to be here."

At the same time, Morgan said, "I'm really happy to be competing—and honored." Morgan's trip to China for the 1999 Worlds lasted two weeks. It was the longest time she had ever been away from her family.

Like all her teammates, she was disappointed by the team's sixth-place showing. She was even more upset by her fall off the beam in team competition. "I don't know what happened on beam," she said. "You can say it's first Worlds jitters, but not really, because I've been that nervous before. I think my series [of moves] was completely straight. It made me so mad. I fell off the beam, and I was like, 'C'mon!' I was completely straight."

Still, the World Championships meet was a wonderful experience for Morgan. She loved seeing the sights in China, especially the Great Wall. Climbing up it, Morgan said, "was one of the hardest things I've ever done in my life."

Morgan began the year 2000 on the upswing. At her first meet of the year, the RCA Challenge, she finished a very respectable fourth in the all-around. Coach Mary Lee Tracy believes more good things lie ahead for Morgan. "Morgan is a creeper," Mary Lee told *International Gymnast* magazine. "She might not have anything that wows you, but she's clean, she hits, she loves what she does, and she's a real competitor. I think she will continue, all the way through 2000, creeping."

Her biggest challenge, Morgan admits, "is overcoming my doubts. I had to learn to believe in myself." She credits Mary Lee with helping her do that. She also gets support from her friendship with Alyssa Beckerman and Jennie Thompson, her teammates at Cincinnati Gymnastics Academy. "We are so close," Morgan says. "It's always just the three of us. We know each other's needs and are able to help one another when we're struggling."

According to Mary Lee Tracy, Morgan is something of a perfectionist who takes her gymnastics very seriously. In fact, Mary Lee sometimes tells Morgan to lighten up! But she also realizes that Morgan's determination and dedication are what make her a world-class competitor.

In her spare time, Morgan relaxes by watching TV and videos. She enjoys going to the movies, too, especially those with her favorite actor, Brad Pitt, and listens to music by alternative rock bands such as Nirvana, Pearl Jam, and Green Day. She also likes bicycling and spending time with her family. Hobbies include collecting coffee mugs and coins from all over the world, something her travels help her to do. She loves hearing from fans and has been trying to answer all her mail, but with her growing fame and success, that has become far more difficult.

With the arrival of the 2000 season, perhaps her most important one yet, Morgan set her sights on her upcoming meets and on Sydney. "It's hard not to think about it, but you can't think about what's going to happen eight months from now," she said after her fourth-place finish at the 2000 RCA Gymnastics Challenge. "I still have a few more meets to go." Always optimistic, Morgan fervently hopes to make it to Sydney, but says, "If I don't, I'll just see what happens."

COMPETITION HIGHLIGHTS

2000 Visa American Cup, 2nd AA and FX, 4th BB and UB

1999 World Championships, 6th team

1999 World Team Trials, 5th AA

1999 U.S. Gymnastics Championships, 7th AA, 3rd UB, 6th BB

1999 Pan American Games, 2nd team, 1st AA, 3rd UB

1999 China Dual, 1st team

1998 U.S. Championships, 1st AA, 1st UB, 1st FX (junior division)

1998 Junior Pan Am Championships, 1st team, 2nd AA

1997 U.S. Gymnastics Championships, 12th AA

AMERICAN GYMNASTS CLOSE-UPS:
Jennie Thompson

In most sports, an eighteen-year-old is a rookie just beginning her career. But in gymnastics, an athlete of eighteen is usually a veteran with years of experience and competition behind her. Having turned eighteen in 1999, Jennie Thompson was one of the oldest members of the 1999 Worlds team and easily the most experienced. She's been a world-class gymnast since 1991, when as a ten-year-old, she won three gold medals in her first major international meet. By the time she was twelve, she was already the best junior gymnast in America and the youngest all-around winner in U.S. gymnastics history. Since that time she's proved to be one of the most consistent and dependable members of the national team.

Her years of experience, plus her talent and determination, have made her a valued and respected member of the team. Her upbeat attitude and leadership qualities have made her a natural choice as team captain at important meets such as the Pan Am Games. Her presence is a steadying and unifying influence on the team as well as an inspiration to her younger teammates.

After nearly a decade of competition, Jennie still loves what she does and maintains as much enthusiasm for her sport as she did at the beginning. "It's cool," she says. "Nobody else can flip and fly through the air like we do."

Jennie Leigh Thompson was born on July 29, 1981, in Wichita Falls, Texas. She's one of two children; the other is her older brother, Matthew. Her mother, Samm, works in a bank and was once a secretary to baseball great Mickey Mantle. Her father, Dennis, works in Houston while the rest of the family lives in Cincinnati. He flies in to see the family on a regular basis.

Jennie began gymnastics classes when she was five. She was a quick learner, too. By the time she was seven, she had mastered moves that many older gymnasts in her gym would not even attempt. Jennie's inspirations were Nadia Comaneci, Mary Lou Retton, and later, Shannon Miller. She currently is a member of Cincinnati Gymnastics Academy, working with Mary Lee Tracy.

At age ten, Jennie competed at her first major international meet, the 1991 Copa Elite competition in Monterrey, Mexico. The event marked the arrival of a bright new star. Jennie took first place in the all-around, balance beam, and uneven bars. A year later she became a member of the U.S. National Team and made an instant impression on the gymnastics world. Just eleven years old, she won three gold medals and two silver medals at the 1992 Junior Pan Am Games in São Paulo, Brazil. That same year she became the youngest event champion in history as she tied for first in the floor exercise at the 1992 Junior National Championships in Columbus, Ohio. And that's not the only "youngest" attached to Jennie's list of achievements. By winning the junior national all-around title in 1993, Jennie became the youngest woman champion in American gymnastics history. She added to her growing medal collection with two more golds—in beam and floor exercise—and a bronze in the all-around at the Junior Pacific Alliance Championships in Canberra, Australia. The next year, Jennie traveled to Saint Petersburg, Russia, for the Goodwill Games where she was the youngest competitor of all.

She competed as a senior at the 1994 U.S. Gymnastics Championships. Her performance— fourth in the all-around and floor, and third on beam—qualified her to try for a place on the

1994 Worlds team. Jennie was ruled ineligible, however, because she was too young.

In 1995 Jennie was plagued by a foot injury and had to wear a heavy cast for weeks. It was a frustrating time for the fourteen-year-old gymnast, and it would be a year before she was back at full strength. When she had recovered enough to begin training, she set out to perfect additional moves and add dance elements to her floor exercise. With her already strong tumbling and acrobatic skills, Jennie hoped the new moves would add sophistication and style to her already impressive performances.

By 1996, Jennie was back in the swing of things and ready to compete again. Her fifth-place finish at the American Classic in April was followed by a gold medal performance in the all-around at the U.S. Classic the next month. At that meet, she scored 9.5 or higher in each event and edged out future Olympian and Mag Seven member Amanda Borden, 77.110 to 76.890. Jennie earned a trip to the 1996 Olympic trials, but her ninth-place performance was two places shy of an Olympic berth.

Not making the 1996 Olympic team was a major disappointment for the fifteen-year-old. Jennie told reporters she would have retired after the Olympics if she had made the team, but instead she set her sights on the 2000 Games. To help achieve her goal, she decided it was time for a coaching change. Based on the recommendations of Olympians Amanda Borden and Jaycie Phelps, Jennie headed to the Cincinnati Gymnastics Academy and began training with Mary Lee Tracy, the assistant coach of the 1996 Olympic team.

Jennie grew taller and more muscular in the next year or so. Her skills continued to grow as she and Mary Lee Tracy concentrated on improving her form. In 1997 she finished seventh in the all-around at the National Championships and qualified for the team heading to Lausanne, Switzerland, for the World Championships. At sixteen, she was finally age-eligible and healthy enough to make a Worlds team. While the team's sixth-place score was a disappointment, the trip proved to be a valuable experience for Jennie.

Her growth and sophistication were evident at the 1998 U.S. Classic. She captured the all-around gold by more than two full points, a huge margin in gymnastics competitions. She earned a total score of over 38.0, a difficult feat under the new code of points that went into effect in 1997.

Things looked even brighter in 1999. At the

American Cup, Jennie surprised everyone by upsetting favorites Vanessa Atler and Elena Produnova of Russia, and taking first place in the all-around competition and uneven bars. The victory lifted Jennie's spirits and gave her renewed faith in herself. "It was really good for me," she said. "It boosted my self-confidence and reminded me where I'm at and set me up for the rest of the year."

She was named captain of the U.S. team heading to the 1999 Pan Am Games. Jennie helped the team win the silver medal in the team competition, and she took third place in the all-around competition. She was in contention for the gold medal, but a fall on the beam in the final rotation dropped her into third. Later she was forced to withdraw from the Event Finals when she landed awkwardly after a vault and aggravated a sore ankle. With both the National Championships and the Worlds approaching, coach Mary Lee Tracy could not risk further injury to Jennie, so she pulled her from the competition. "I'm kind of disappointed," Jennie admitted, "but I think it's a good learning experience for me to see all the other gymnasts from other countries and see what kind of skills they're doing."

The Pam Am Games were important for other reasons, too. The event boosted team spirit and allowed friendships to develop between team members. "It was exciting," Jennie noted, "because it's a chance to compete as a team, which we don't often do. It helps to build our World Championships team and Olympic team."

Jennie was back in good health and good form at the 1999 U.S. Gymnastics Championships. She felt relaxed and tried to stay focused on what she knew she could do. The strategy worked, and she won bronze on beam and tied for the gold medal on uneven bars. "I knew I could do it," she said later. "I came away with two medals. I am very happy about how I did tonight. I didn't put any pressure on myself and it really worked out for me. I am ready to peak at Worlds, so I am going home to practice very hard." She did admit, however, "I'm not where I want to be yet in any event."

At the trials, Jennie established a narrow lead over Elise Ray and her Cincinnati teammate Alyssa Beckerman in the preliminaries. Unfortunately, she was plagued by an upper respiratory infection and acute sinusitis, so she had to withdraw from the trials. Luckily, her showings earlier in the season allowed her to petition onto the Worlds team.

Like all gymnasts, Jennie has gone through

occasional moments of doubt. Her coach, Mary Lee Tracy, explained, "I think it took a while for her to believe in herself. I believe her hard work and continuous perseverance have paid off. I just think that she believes now that she can do it and that she's one of the top kids in the country. It takes believing in yourself. It doesn't matter if I believe in her or anyone else believes in her. She's got to believe in herself, and I think she does now."

Jennie has earned a reputation as a hard worker and tireless trainer. "She's a work-horse," her former coach Peggy Liddick commented. "She works at a very high level all the time."

At the same time, Jennie doesn't obsess about gymnastics. A visitor to her room once noticed that there were far more cow collectibles than gymnastics mementos. (Jennie collects toys, stuffed animals, tablecloths, and other things that have cow-related themes and designs.)

While gymnastics is very important to her, Jennie is certainly not obsessed with winning medals. "I just like doing the sport," she stated. "It's fun for me now, a lot more than it was before. I just like going in the gym every day and working out."

Jennie has always been one of the most

popular gymnasts on the national team, and she appreciates the support she has gotten through thick and thin from her fans. "I think having fans helps," she said. "I'm not going to say it affects my performance, but it pumps you up if you know that people are out there cheering for you and supporting you."

She is particularly close to her gym mates, Alyssa Beckerman and Morgan White. The three are more friends than rivals. "We totally get along," Jennie explained. "We know each other so well that we are kind of like sisters. It helps to have them compete with me because we really push each other."

Off the floor, Jennie spends her spare time shopping at the mall, in-line skating, swimming, using the computer, and watching movies. She likes reading and listening to the music of the Dave Matthews Band and Garth Brooks. She attended public schools all through her career before graduating in spring 1999. Her favorite subjects were English and math. She loves animals and has had three dogs named Sissy, Cinnamon, and Scruffy, and two cats named Muffin and Snowball.

Jennie is hoping for another shot at the Olympic team in 2000, but not making the 1996 team taught her a valuable lesson. "I learned that life goes on," she says. "Last time it was a lot harder for me because I really wanted to be there and I didn't know anything else. Hopefully I'll make it to Sydney, but if not, I think I'll be okay with where I'm at and who I am."

COMPETITION HIGHLIGHTS

1999   World Championships, 6th team

1999   U.S. Gymnastics Championships, 3rd AA and BB, 1st UB

1999   Pan Am Games, 2nd team, 3rd AA

1999   American Classic, Pan Am Trials, 2nd AA

1999   Visa American Cup, 1st AA and UB

1997   World Gymnastics Championships, 6th team

1996   U.S. Gymnastics Championships, 8th AA, 6th UB and BB, 3rd FX

1994   Goodwill Games, 4th team

1993   U.S. Gymnastics Championships, 1st AA (junior division)

1992   U.S. Gymnastics Championships, 7th AA, 1st (tie) FX (junior division)

1992   Junior Pan Am Games, 1st AA, team and BB, 2nd UB and FX

AMERICAN GYMNASTS CLOSE-UPS:
Alyssa Beckerman

The year 1999 marked a breakout season for Alyssa Beckerman. While she had shown great potential in previous years, most of her finishes at major meets had been shy of the top ten. In late 1998 and early 1999, though, Alyssa began to gain momentum. She blossomed into a consistent medal-winning gymnast, and her season culminated in two fine performances at the 1999 U.S. Gymnastics Championships and the World Team Trials.

When she was denied a trip to Tianjin for the World Championships because of her broken wrist, Alyssa caught a tough break, but she cannot be counted out for a shot at an Olympic berth in 2000.

Alyssa brings a lot to the national team. She provides a solid and dependable presence on uneven bars, her best event. She is known for her clean presentation, beautiful lines, and pretty and polished hand movements. Alyssa is also a promising performer in the all-around, and a well-liked team player. One of her most important contributions is in the team spirit department. Once described as a performer with "a 1,000-megawatt smile," Alyssa is valued for her upbeat attitude and her ability to make her teammates laugh.

Not surprisingly, her favorite competitions are team events. "I get very excited at those competitions, and I love the sport," Alyssa says enthusiastically. "I love gymnastics. I love what I do. I like to bring that feeling with me when I compete and when I cheer for others."

Alyssa Beckerman was born in Long Branch, New Jersey, on January 23, 1981. Her father, Howard, is an inventor, and she has two brothers—Mathew, who's four years older, and younger brother Jared, a computer whiz who created Alyssa's Web site.

She started with local New Jersey gyms, but later moved to Wyoming, Ohio with Jared and her mother, Melanie, to train with Mary Lee Tracy at the Cincinnati Gymnastics Academy. (Her father stayed at home in New Jersey to run his business. He flies out to see his family every few weeks.) However, Alyssa still considers Middletown, New Jersey, her home.

Alyssa's debut as an Elite gymnast came in 1996 when she finished eighth in the all-around competition at the American Classic in

Tulsa, Oklahoma. That year she competed as a junior at the U.S. Gymnastics Championships, placing twenty-fifth in the all-around. In 1997 she became a national team member. In the first few years of her Elite career, Alyssa didn't win many medals, but by 1998 she was showing tremendous progress as she improved her scores in every event.

At her second major international meet, the 1998 Ecoair Gymnastics Cup in Zoetermeer, Netherlands, she won a silver medal in the all-around and bronze medals in beam and floor exercise. It was her best showing up to that point. At the 1998 National Championships, she continued her winning ways as she won a silver medal in uneven bars and finished in the top ten in beam, floor exercise, and the all-around.

Alyssa was a member of the American team that won the silver medal at the 1999 International Team Championships in Richmond, Virginia. She made a strong showing, too, in the all-around with a seventh-place finish. She improved on that performance at the American Classic meet, where she won bronze medals in the all-around and floor exercise, and took the silver on beam. She just missed capturing another medal with a fourth-place finish on bars. That standout performance earned her a place on the team heading to the Pan Am Games in Canada that summer.

Alyssa was glad to be a member of the Pan Am Games team, and was especially happy to be there with Morgan White and Jennie Thompson. That made the competition a special experience for Alyssa: "Competing with my teammates from Cincinnati Gymnastics Academy really builds my confidence and makes me feel like I am back at home training. It puts me in a comfort zone."

At the 1999 U.S. Gymnastics Championships she turned in strong sets on beam and bars, and ended up in fourth place in the all-around. In the Event Finals, she tied her teammate Morgan White for the bronze medal on bars.

Alyssa had her heart set on competing at the World Team Trials in Kansas City, so she trained hard after the Nationals. A week before the trials, she injured her wrist while practicing her vault. When the pain did not subside, Alyssa had X-rays taken. Nothing could be seen on the X-rays, so Alyssa headed to Kansas City.

She did well in the World Team Trials despite the pain in her wrist. But in the finals, she slipped off the beam, and the resulting score, 8.825, suddenly put her place on the Worlds team in serious jeopardy. "When I dismounted, I realized just how bad that mistake was. It really kept me hanging on a thread there," she recalled. The suspense was almost too much.

"Mary Lee hugged me and she knew it, too," Alyssa remembered. "She knew it was crunch time. She basically told me that we would just have to wait and see what happens. She told me the whole time, from the beginning, not to look at the scoreboard, not to look at what everyone else was doing, just to focus on myself. Basically that's what I was doing, so I really had no idea just how close it was.

"It was really intense," Alyssa continued. She couldn't even watch the rest of the event. She ran to the locker room and changed her clothes right after her beam routine. "I couldn't bear to watch the rest of the competition," she said.

She was sitting in the stands when she saw the women's program director from USA Gymnastics, Kathy Kelly, hugging and congratulating Jeanette Antolin and Elise Ray, whose scores had qualified them for the Worlds team.

When the final scores were posted, it became clear that Alyssa had edged out Jamie Dantzscher for the last spot on the team. Alyssa spotted Kathy Kelly searching for her. "I saw her looking for me and I knew. I was so happy. It was like the best feeling of my life."

Alyssa said afterwards, "I'm ecstatic. I'm

beside myself. I can't believe this is happening. My dreams are coming true."

A week later the dream became a nightmare. After the trials, Alyssa's wrist still hurt and she was told to get an MRI (magnetic resonance imaging). She soon learned that doctors had found a tiny fracture in her wrist, an injury that was more serious than it felt. Alyssa's wrist was quite delicate, and if it broke, it would require surgery and as much as six months of rehabilitation. Alyssa and her coach, Mary Lee Tracy, realized they had no choice but to skip the Worlds.

"This isn't like a stress fracture, where you can just get through," Mary Lee explained. "The doctors couldn't believe she'd made it through the [Kansas City] meet. Right now it's better for her not to risk six months out of the gym."

Jamie Dantzscher took Alyssa's place, and Morgan White was named alternate. Alyssa took it well, although she thought it was "weird" to have worked so hard for something only to have it taken away. Still, she felt good knowing that her teammate Morgan White would now get a chance to go to the Worlds as alternate. That attitude was typical of Alyssa's unselfish perspective and good nature. She was still happy with her successes and all she had achieved in the 1999 season.

"This year I learned from my mistakes, and I learned how to focus better," she noted as she recuperated. "I'm still learning. I still need to learn. This is all a part of the process. This is like a stepping-stone for next year. It has really been a great year for me. I had a great American Classic and a really good experience leading up to World Team Trials. Getting the experience of competing with national-caliber athletes and dealing with pressure is so important. You learn to rise to the occasion very quickly."

In her gymnastics, Alyssa is known more for her finesse than for her strength. She's solid on beam and strong on bars, and she shows a lot of style on the floor. If she can be more consistent, develop more powerful and difficult moves in both vault and the tumbling portion of her floor exercise, she could be a contender for a medal in Sydney.

Mary Lee Tracy credits Alyssa's lighthearted attitude for bringing a much-needed sense of fun to practices and competitions. "Sometimes we'll be really serious about something," Mary Lee observes, "and she'll say something, and all of a sudden you're cracking up."

In her spare time, Alyssa enjoys in-line skating, shopping, surfing the Net, and listening to music. She relaxes by watching movies and TV comedies like *Friends*, *Seinfeld*, *Frasier*, and *South Park*. An avid reader, her favorite book is *The Diary of Anne Frank*.

Alyssa was an excellent student in high school, maintaining a 3.75 grade point average. It's hardly surprising that as the daughter of an inventor, Alyssa's favorite subject was science. She plans to take a year off to train for the 2000 Olympics. She's signed a letter of intent to go to UCLA, where she hopes to begin classes in the fall of 2000. She hasn't made up her mind about a career, but has said that she might like to be an actor or a singer.

COMPETITION HIGHLIGHTS

2000   Spieth-Sogipa Cup, 1st team and AA

1999   World Team Trials, 3rd AA

1999   U.S. Gymnastics Championships, 4th AA, 3rd UB

1999   Pan American Games, 2nd team

1999   American Classic, Pan Am Trials, 3rd AA

1999   International Team Championships, 2nd team

1998   U.S. Gymnastics Championships, 8th AA, 2nd UB, 8th BB, 7th FX

1998   U.S. Classic, 4th AA and UB, 5th BB

1998   American Classic, 10th AA and UB, 4th BB (tie)

1998   Ecoair Gymnastics Cup, 2nd AA, 7th V, 4th UB, 3rd BB and FX

Jeanette Antolin

As *International Gymnast* magazine once put it, Jeanette Antolin's career "has been a series of almosts." While she has turned in more than her share of medal-winning performances, she's never gotten anywhere near as much attention as some of her teammates. She was an alternate on the 1997 Worlds team, but never actually got to compete. She earned gold medals at a variety of important meets here and overseas, but except for two bronze medals, similar success has so far eluded her at the National Championships. In 1999, when her chances seemed brightest for a breakout at the Nationals, an injury just weeks before the event forced her to withdraw.

Jeanette's name can usually be found among the top five or six finishers at most meets she enters, and her record has put her very near the top of the women's gymnastics world. Her career has been gaining momentum for the past two years, and 2000 may finally see her rise above "almosts" and win the recognition she deserves.

Jeanette herself has noted, "It always seems like I just make it or I'm right at the edge. If you're not in the top three, it seems like you're always overlooked, so I'm just hoping to move up." Even though her name is becoming better known to gymnastics fans, she observed that "There's still that space after they announce my name where people are, like, 'Now wait, who is she?'"

Fans may not be asking that question too much longer. A consistent and steady gymnast, Netters, as she is known to friends and fans, has excellent skills and original moves that give her a style all her own. Thanks also to her fashion flair on the floor, she has a look and a presence that have attracted an army of admirers who follow her career via the Internet.

Born on October 5, 1981, Jeanette grew up in Paradise, a small town in northern California. She's one of three children born to Orlando, who works in construction, and Nola Antolin, a secretary and teacher. A talent for gymnastics runs in the family. Her brother, Gilbert, was a gymnast, and her older sister, Katie, won a gymnastics scholarship at Cal State, Fullerton, and was a member of the Junior National team in 1993. In fact, it was

Katie, just a year and a half older, who inspired Jeanette to take up gymnastics.

The three Antolin children were always tumbling and jumping around the house. When Katie was young, her parents enrolled her in a beginning gymnastics class. Before long, four-year-old Jeanette wanted to take up gymnastics as well. "I was the little one in the family," Jeanette remembered. "We would go watch Katie, and I wanted to be like her."

It was just a hobby at first, but it soon became a passion. Both sisters progressed rapidly, and some said they had the talent to become future Olympians, with the right training. When Jeanette was nine, the family realized that she could not get that level of coaching in Paradise. So in 1991 the family moved to Huntington Beach in southern California and joined the SCATS (Southern California Acro Team) gym, which had been run by Don Peters, one of the coaches of the 1984 Olympic team.

Peters had retired from coaching, but one day he dropped by the gym and was struck by Jeanette's ability and style. He saw tremendous potential and was so impressed that he decided to come out of retirement to work with her. From the very start, Peters noticed two traits in Jeanette: competitiveness and determination. Sister Katie seemed to have a natural athletic ability, Peters recalled, and "Jeanette had a lot of heart and real dedication. She loved to compete and perform." He had seen many gymnasts who had moments of hesitation as their turn came, but he noticed that Jeanette usually couldn't wait to perform.

Jeanette and her sister flourished at SCATS. They trained together for years, and Katie was always an inspiration rather than the object of envy to her younger sister. "It's not that I wanted to beat her. I just wanted to get to her level," Jeanette recalled.

She did and soon exceeded it. Jeanette and her coach decided it was time to raise her international profile, and in 1994 she traveled to Avignon, France, to compete in her first international meet, the City of Popes event. She finished fifteenth in the all-around. In the next four years she would compete regularly at meets in China, Switzerland, and Italy. (International meets are important not only for the experience but also for demonstrating their routines and skills for foreign judges, which can help at later meets.) She was sometimes the only American woman at those meets. As a result, Jeanette has more international experience than some of her teammates.

In 1995 she became a member of the U.S. National Team. Competing as a junior, she finished ninth in the all-around and sixth on bars at the 1995 Nationals. With that performance, she became one of the top ten junior gymnasts. The next year she improved still further, finishing fifth in the all-around and tying for the gold medal at the important U.S. Classic. In 1997 she graduated to senior status and took home a bronze medal in vault at the U.S. Championships. In the all-around she avoided major mistakes and falls, but finished only tenth, which indicated that she needed to incorporate more difficult elements into her routines to get higher scores. Still, based on her 1997 showing, Jeanette was named an alternate on the 1997 Worlds team.

Improving steadily, Jeanette stepped up her international competition schedule in 1998. At the 1998 Grand Prix in Zurich, Switzerland, she won the bronze in the uneven bars, her favorite event. She won the all-around at the Como Cup meet in Italy and took the gold on bars, vault, and floor and a silver in the all-around at the Monte Fiore Friendly Cup competition also in Italy.

On the home front, she took a silver and a bronze in bars and beam at the 1998 American Classic. But at the 1998 U.S. Gymnastics Championships, she competed with a foot injury and was not at her best. She had a difficult first day, and the pain in her foot made vaulting and tumbling in floor exercise quite difficult, but Jeanette would not quit. Although she recovered her form later, she ended up in sixth place in the all-around. She did, however, take the bronze medal on bars in the Event Finals.

Jeanette began 1999 in a winning mode. As a contingent of family members and friends cheered her on, she finished fourth at the American Classic, Pan Am Trials in Pomona, California. The results earned her a place on the team that would go to the Pan Am Games later in the year. She had made great progress working with coach Don Peters, but her selection as a Pan Am Games team member inspired her to work even harder. "Since the Pan Am trials, I've added a new skill on each apparatus," she said at the time. "Training has been great." One of the new skills she had mastered was a Jaeger salto in a layout position, a move no other woman in the world was doing in competition.

As the fourth-ranked gymnast in the country, Jeanette was eager to improve her status as the 1999 U.S. Gymnastics Championships approached, and she trained hard. But two weeks before the Nationals, she fell headfirst off the uneven bars and sprained her neck. She felt okay later that night, but when she woke up the next morning, she could hardly move. The injury forced her to drop out of the Nationals. Luckily she was able to petition her way into the World Team Trials.

As the trials neared, Jeanette stepped up her training, trying to make up for lost time. Missing the championships had put her at a disadvantage because Worlds team positions would be awarded based on a combination of scores at the trials and earlier scores from Nationals. "I felt a little bit of pressure because everyone else had their starting scores from championships and knew what they had to do, and I wasn't sure how good I needed to be," she observed. "I just tried to brush the pressure off and go out there and do what I had to do."

Jeanette rose to the occasion with one of her best all-around performances. She finished second to Elise Ray in the all-around and had consistently high marks in all four events, scoring 9.637 in floor, 9.537 on beam, 9.462 in vault, and 9.25 on bars. She had unveiled a new floor exercise routine, set to music from *Gone With the Wind*, that drew enthusiastic applause from the audience.

"I'm thrilled beyond words," Jeanette said afterward. "It's amazing. I showed more consistency and really improved my floor routine. This was only the second time I've ever done that routine, and it took all my adrenaline. I thought the crowd support was awesome." Jeanette added, "I love showing off in front of the crowd."

Jeanette, her coach, and her choreographer had searched for just the right piece of music for her floor exercise. When another coach suggested the *Gone With the Wind* theme, it seemed perfect. Jeanette, Don Peters explains, "has beautiful arms and hands, and I wanted music that would facilitate her using that. We wanted music that would be elegant and beautiful, and I think we found it."

Jeanette was very much looking forward to the 1999 Worlds and the chance to compete against the world's best. "At the 1997 Worlds, I was an alternate. It was a disappointment because I had to watch from the stands. Now I'm just so excited that I get to go and actually compete. It's a dream come true."

The trip to the Tianjin World Championships would not be Jeanette's first visit to China. She had competed there before, and the experience had not been a pleasant one because of jet lag, poor accommodations, unfamiliar food, and less than ideal facilities. But this time, Jeanette was pleasantly surprised. The hotel was nice, and she was hardly bothered by jet lag at all. She was a bit anxious about competing, though. "I was a little nervous," she admitted. "I always get nervous at competitions, but this one I was a little extra nervous because it was my first Worlds."

While Jeanette didn't place in the top ten in any events in Tianjin, she enjoyed the experience. "It was really fun," she told reporters. "I thought it was going to be a lot more nerve-racking, but it went so quickly."

Looking toward 2000, Jeanette's coach, Don Peters, advised her to keep working on her new routines and to keep up her rigorous training. The 2000 season, he said, would provide a proving ground for Jeanette's new routines and give her more time to hone and develop her new skills. One thing Jeanette wanted to do was boost her vault scores by mastering a new and difficult move, a layout Khorkina (named after Russian champion Svetlana Khorkina) that has a 10.0 start value. The goal, Don Peters noted, was to get Jeanette to work on those new moves and nail them well before the summer, and "make her competitive for Sydney."

When the Sydney Games begin in September 2000, Jeanette will be eighteen and hopefully at the peak of her abilities. "It's a letdown sometimes if you're ready and not old enough or if, by the time the Olympics get here, you're too old. But I'll be ready to go. I'm already excited."

Don Peters says Jeanette's strengths are "her elegance, strength, and power." She strives to be original and create a unique style and presence, and is not afraid to try new and difficult moves. "One of Jeanette's great qualities is that she has the courage of a lion and is willing to try anything new," says her coach. "She's very gutsy and not afraid to try new things, even if they are risky. It's one of the reasons she's so easy to work with."

Jeanette is also known for her fashion flair on the floor. After her coach suggested that the long-sleeved leotards worn by most of her teammates made her look shorter, Jeanette traded them for the sleeveless ones that have become her trademark. They also help people remember her better. She owns more than one hundred leotards!

At the SCATS gym, Jeanette is also respected for her kindness, friendliness, and concern for her gym mates, especially the younger ones who hope to follow in her footsteps. "They love her," Peters declared. "If she sees one of the little ones having a bad day, she'll come up and put an arm around them."

"There's not really pressure to succeed," Jeanette commented, "but I feel if I'm going to be up there, I should try my best to be an inspiration to little kids. There are a lot of little girls at my gym. It's important to be a role model for them." She is, in more ways than one. Whenever Jeanette wears a new leotard, all the little girls at the gym rush out to buy the same one, hoping it will bring them good luck.

"I love being somebody everyone looks up to," Jeanette has said. She's also the first Hispanic gymnast on the women's team in more than twenty-five years. That's a particular point of pride for Jeanette. "It's very important to me, not only for myself, but for all Hispanic girls. There aren't many famous Hispanic gymnasts. I can be a good role model."

As far as a career is concerned, Jeanette has mentioned that she might like to work in the field of fashion, cosmetology, or acting someday. "I'm not stuck on gymnastics for life," she noted. "I have a life outside gymnastics. I'm not the kind of person who has a hall of fame on my wall with medals everywhere." She has even occasionally thought about quitting the sport, but when she thinks about how much time and effort she's put into it, the idea passes quickly. As she says, "I've been in this sport for fourteen years, and giving it up just because I had a bad day or something isn't worth it."

Both Jeanette and her coach recognize the need to be well rounded and do normal teenage things, and that's one reason she has attended public high school full-time. Jeanette's schedule allows her to shift training sessions around for school functions, school dances, and dates or to go to clubs with her friends. "I'm a normal kid outside the gym," she says. People who know her describe her as upbeat, cheerful, and quick to laugh.

That doesn't mean she doesn't work hard at gymnastics. She still gets up early and trains for hours most days of the week. "Just the time and responsibility of getting up, going to practice, working your hardest, staying there and giving 100 percent takes a lot out of a person," she says.

In her spare time, Jeanette likes hanging out with friends, dancing, swimming, and shopping. To relax, she enjoys going to the movies or watching TV shows such as *I Love Lucy*, *Friends*, and *South Park*. Music is another interest. Her favorite performers are Britney Spears, the Backstreet Boys, and Lauryn Hill. She collects jewelry and loves buying cosmetics. The gymnasts she admires most are Mary Lou Retton, Lilia Podkopayeva, and the Mag Seven's Dominique Dawes.

She graduated from Marina High School in the spring of 2000 and intends to go to UCLA in 2001, no matter what happens in her gymnastics career. Even if a medal at Sydney is not in the cards, Jeanette will not look for another shot at Olympic gold in 2004. She believes four more years of intense training for the next Olympics would take too much of a physical toll on her body. "If it wasn't meant to be in 2000," she said, "I don't think it was meant to be."

COMPETITION HIGHLIGHTS

1999   World Championships, 6th team

1999   World Team Trials, 2nd AA

1999   Pan Am Games, 2nd team

1999   Visa American Cup, 5th AA (preliminaries)

1998   Grand Prix, Zurich, 3rd UB

1998   Monte Fiore Friendly Cup, 2nd AA, 1st VT, UB, and FX

1998   Como Cup, 1st AA

1998   American Classic, 2nd UB, 3rd BB

1997   World Championships Team (alternate)

1997   U.S. Gymnastics Championships 10th AA, 3rd VT (tie)

1996   U.S. Gymnastics Championships, 5th AA (junior division)

AMERICAN GYMNASTS CLOSE-UPS:
Jamie Dantzscher

Gymnastics is a family affair for 1999 national uneven bars champion Jamie Dantzscher. She is one of seven children, four of whom are gymnasts. Jamie's younger twin sisters, Jalynne and Janelle, who will be thirteen in 2000, are rising young gymnasts in their own right.

The kids in Jamie's family—Jennifer, Joanne, Jeremy, Johnny, and the twins—were always an active, energetic bunch who grew up tumbling and playing sports together. Jamie, the third oldest, wasn't the first Dantzscher to take up gymnastics (an older sister was), but she has carried the family name to heights unimagined in 1989, when seven-year-old Jamie used her tumbling talents to take off on a medal-winning gymnastics journey.

Jamie showed potential early, winning medals in junior competitions by the time she was thirteen, but not until recent years did Jamie reach the top echelon of Elite gymnasts. Her progress has been sure and steady, and each year she has surpassed her previous performances. In the three national championships from 1997 to 1999, Jamie rose from bronze medal finishes to silver and finally to gold in 1999. Known as an uneven bars standout, Jamie is a well-rounded gymnast with solid skills on vault and floor exercise as well, which makes her valuable in team competition.

Jamie Dantzscher was born on May 2, 1982, in Canoga Park, California, and grew up in nearby Palmdale. Her mother, Joyce, works part-time in a pharmacy, and her father, John, is a grocery store manager.

Jamie's older sister, Jennifer, was the first family member to take up the sport, and it was only a matter of time before seven-year-old Jamie asked to be enrolled in gymnastics classes. At AV Twisters, a gym near their Palmdale home, both Jennifer and Jamie showed promise early on. It was there that Jamie met her future teammate and close friend, Vanessa Atler. One day, Jennifer, Jamie, and Vanessa were sent to a gym in Covina for what was supposed to be a brief visit to learn some new choreography for their floor exercise programs. At the other gym, the Charter Oak Gliders, the girls met coaches Beth and Steve Rybacki. Impressed by the Rybackis, Jamie and Jennifer decided to switch full-time to Charter Oak.

Moving to another gym forced the Dantzscher family to make major changes in their lives. It was no easy matter shuttling Jamie, and later her twin sisters, from Palmdale over the California freeways to Charter Oak. The Dantzschers sometimes drove more than 5,000 miles each month on trips to and from the gym. Not long after joining Charter Oak, Jamie and her mother moved to neighboring San Dimas while the rest of the family stayed in Palmdale. Even with the move, however, Joyce Dantzscher had to make several round trips each week from Covina to Palmdale for work or to drive her daughter back to see the rest of the family. But the sacrifices paid off as Jamie rose to Elite status under the guidance of the Rybackis. By age twelve, she was competing at the national level and finished fourth in the junior all-around at the 1994 U.S. Classic in Palm Springs, California.

The year 1995 was a good one for the thirteen-year-old Californian. She finished in the top eight in the all-around in four major meets, including sixth place at the 1995 National Championships. She might have finished higher had it not been for a disastrous bars routine in which she fell three times. The 1995 Nationals were also noteworthy for Jamie as she took first in junior division vault. She also redeemed herself on bars in the Event Finals as she returned to form and captured the silver medal. At another major international meet, the 1995 International Junior Championships, she took the silver in floor exercises behind Vanessa Atler.

The next year, Jamie fell to seventh place in the junior all-around at the Nationals, but she continued to gain experience with solid showings at several important meets, including the American Classic, where she finished fourth in the junior all-around. But the highlight of her year was a trip to France to compete in the City of Popes competition. The meet, in which Jamie won the gold medal in the all-around and floor exercise, and a silver in vault, remains one of Jamie's favorite moments in her career.

Entering the senior ranks, Jamie won a bronze medal at the 1997 U.S. Championships. She scored 9.25 or better in vault, bars, and floor, winning acclaim for her stylish floor routine and her solid performance on bars. She also unveiled several new moves, but a fall off the beam and the resulting 8.350 score dropped her into sixth in the all-around.

Jamie's all-around scores still qualified her for a place on the 1997 Worlds team, and she really wanted to compete. Like Vanessa Atler, however, she was ineligible because she was too young. "I don't know if we would have won," she said, "but it was kind of unfair because they didn't take the top six from championships. It was kind of upsetting, but I knew that was going to happen."

Still, the 1997 National Championships meet was one Jamie's best performances up till then, and it gave her confidence a big boost. The meet was, in Steve Rybacki's words, "Jamie's coming-out party." Another highlight that year for Jamie was her trip to Adelaide, Australia, for the Foxtel Gymnastics Challenge. There she not only won a silver in floor exercise but also helped the American squad take the team gold.

She continued her winning ways at the American Classic in Orlando, Florida, in February 1998, where she took the silver medal in floor exercises and tied Dominique Dawes for the gold in vault. Her all-around score, 37.237, was a point behind winner Kristen Maloney and good for second place.

In June of 1998, Jamie had arthroscopic surgery to repair a nagging wrist injury. Later that summer she had recovered enough to capture another silver medal at the Nationals. But because of her wrist and back problems, Jamie was not at the top of her form, especially on beam, where she had to cut back on some of the difficult moves she had done previously. Perhaps as a result of her physical problems, she slipped to ninth place in the all-around.

Jamie resumed her climb in 1999. At the American Classic she won silver in vault and bronze on bars and rose to fifth in the all-around. She traveled to Asia for the China Dual event, in which she contributed to the team's first-place showing. She was also a member of the U.S. team that took the silver at the 1999 International Team Championships.

Despite her steady progress, Jamie was having some doubts about her future as the 1999 Nationals neared. Jamie believed she needed to make some changes if she was to take her performance to the next level and have a shot at an Olympic medal. Questions about her goals and her career had been nagging her for months, Jamie later admitted. Jamie finally made a difficult decision.

After bidding a tearful farewell to longtime coaches Steve and Beth Rybacki and to her friend Vanessa Atler, Jamie moved to the

Southern California Acro Team gymnastics club. In her first meet representing the new gym, the Pan Am Games, Jamie introduced some new moves on beam and the floor. She finished fifth in floor exercise, seventh on beam, and eighth in the all-around, but later admitted that she was not 100 percent satisfied with her performance. "Right now I'm not as ready as I'd like to be for competition. But that's okay, because I want to be more ready for championships and World Team Trials—the Worlds. You want to peak at Worlds."

Jamie eventually returned to the Charter Oak gym, where her younger sisters had continued to train. There were no hard feelings. SCATS's Don Peters complimented Jamie, saying she was "very gifted, very nice, and very sincere. She has tremendous ability."

Jamie's crowning moment came at the 1999 U.S. Gymnastics Championships in Sacramento, California, when her 9.675 score on uneven bars placed her in a tie for first place with Jennie Thompson in the Event Finals. "I was excited, especially to win a gold on bars," she said. "I think it's my best event and my favorite, so that made me feel good."

She gives a lot of credit to her Charter Oak teammates, especially Vanessa Atler. "Vanessa inspires me a lot. So does everyone here. They're so determined—everyone wants to win."

Jamie was eager to compete at the World Team Trials because it would give her another chance to be on a Worlds team. This time she was old enough and had high hopes of making the China-bound team.

In the finals, Jamie gave a great effort, scoring 9.418 in vault and a 9.762 in an impressive floor exercise performance. She was strong on bars, but had a few shaky moments on beam. When the final scores were tabulated, she was in fourth place, behind Elise Ray, Jeanette Antolin, and Alyssa Beckerman— good enough to earn the alternate spot on the Worlds team.

When Alyssa Beckerman's broken wrist caused her to withdraw, Jamie got to compete after all. She didn't know quite what to expect from her first Worlds. "When you picture your dream of going to Worlds," she said, "you picture this whole thing, and now that I'm here, it's just like another meet. I thought it would be bigger. I mean it is big, but I thought it was going to be huge."

Jamie's performance at the World Championships match was marred by a fall off the uneven bars in the preliminary round. Later she admitted that she had the jitters. Like most of her teammates, she didn't qualify for the all-around or the Event Finals, but Jamie was glad to have had the chance to compete at the Worlds level.

Jamie's strengths are her style, her expressive presentation, and her ability to perform difficult moves on a variety of apparatuses. Bars is her favorite event and she has often capped off her set with a show-stopping double-twisting, double back somersault dismount. She's also known for her graceful floor exercise program. Occasionally she has had trouble on beam when doing her most difficult maneuvers, so her coaches simplified some of her routines. Her optimism, sunny disposition, and team spirit have made her well-liked among her fellow gymnasts and a valuable member of the team.

Jamie looks up to the Magnificent Seven's Shannon Miller, Amanda Borden, and Dominique Dawes and to foreign gymnasts such as Henrietta Onodi and Tatiana Gutsu. Of her current teammates, she particularly admires her close friend, Vanessa Atler. "She's awesome," Jamie declared. "Vanessa and I are, like, best friends."

"They've gone through their ups and downs together and they're very close," confirmed Joyce Dantzscher.

Having always been close to her family, Jamie treasures the time she spends with them. One of her happiest memories is of Christmas 1988, when she was just six. The whole family went on vacation together in the California mountains. They enjoyed sledding, snowball fights, and just being together. "We had the greatest time," Jamie remembered.

Jamie attended public school and graduated from San Dimas High School in 2000. She won a gymnastics scholarship to UCLA, where she plans to take courses that will lead to a career as a teacher or an actress.

When she's not practicing, Jamie enjoys listening to the music of Britney Spears, Sugar Ray, and the Backstreet Boys. She's a fan of such TV shows as *Friends* and *The Simpsons*, and any movie starring Jim Carrey, Tom Cruise, or Julia Roberts. Her hobbies include writing poetry, drawing, playing keyboards, shopping, and playing cards. She has three pets, a black miniature pinscher named Little Bit, a German shepherd named Kendle, and a cat named Mickey.

To those who hope to follow in her footsteps and start a gymnastics career, Jamie offers this advice: "Just work hard and have fun." That philosophy seems to be working just fine for Jamie herself.

COMPETITION HIGHLIGHTS

1999   World Championships, 6th team

1999   U.S. Gymnastics Championships, 5th AA, 1st UB (tie), 4th FX

1999   Pan Am Games, 2nd team

1999   American Classic, 5th AA, 2nd V, 3rd UB, 5th FX

1999   International Team Championships, 2nd team

1998   U.S. Gymnastics Championships, 9th AA, 6th V, 2nd FX

1998   American Classic, 2nd AA and FX,, 1st V, 6th UB

1998   International Team Championships, 1st team

1997   U.S. Gymnastics Championships, 6th AA, 3rd UB

1997   American Classic, 2nd AA

A Day in the Life of a Champion Gymnast

B ecoming a champion gymnast is no easy task. It takes years of practice, dedication, and a total commitment to the sport. Many young gymnasts begin training when they are three and four years old. While most teenage girls are busy with school, social life, shopping, and hobbies, the young women on the American gymnastics team may spend thirty-five hours a week in the gym, week in and week out, endlessly practicing their moves and trying to master new ones in their quest to become Elite gymnasts.

Kristen Maloney has been known to train for thirty to thirty-five hours a week, often for six hours a day. She spends an hour warming up with conditioning exercises and dance, then spends an hour each on beam and bars, forty-five minutes on vault, and forty-five minutes practicing her tumbling. Then she finishes with more conditioning and strength exercises.

During her school years, Kristen's training began around 1:30 P.M. and continued until 7:00 P.M. In summer when school was out, she hit the gym at 6:45 A.M. and trained until 11:30. After a 2½-hour lunch break, she worked out for two more hours before quitting for the day.

Kristen's teachers gave her a lot of flexibility as long as she kept up with her work. She preferred to stay close to home and attend public school, rather than having home schooling or leaving home and having private tutors at a faraway gym. "That was important to me," Kristen explained. "I make time for my friends and I don't want to leave public schools. I don't mean to criticize those that do it differently, but those things meant a lot to me and I didn't want to miss out on that. I split my time. Half the time, I'm a normal kid, and half the time I'm a gymnast—who's a normal kid," she said in 1998.

The regimen of a gymnast like Kristen requires a lot of discipline outside the gym. She recalls coming home nearly every night after practice during her high school years and doing little besides eating and homework. "I didn't have any time to do other things, like go out. I did it for so many years it became a habit. It wasn't really that difficult for me," she told *International Gymnast* magazine.

Other gymnasts, like Morgan White, are home-schooled, while still others, like Vanessa Atler, mix tutoring with independent study. These gymnasts may train a little more and have more flexible schedules.

Vanessa Atler and Jamie Dantzscher, when they trained together at the Charter Oak gym, practiced thirty to thirty-five hours a week, anywhere from five to seven hours a day.

Elise Ray, the 1998 uneven bars champion and 1999 floor exercise champion, attended public school and doesn't always do a morning workout. She trains around twenty-five hours a week, which is less than some gymnasts, but when she's in the gym, "she gives 100 percent every day," says her coach, Kelli Hill. Elise Ray offered this account of a typical training day:

5:15 A.M.: wake up for morning practice
5:20: leave for practice ("I eat dry cereal on
    the way. Mom/Dad drives me.")
6:00–7:30: morning practice

7:45–8:25: Mom/Dad drive me to school ("I eat
a bagel or muffin for breakfast in the car.")

8:30–2:00 P.M.: high school classes

2:20: leave for afternoon workout ("I eat a
snack before I leave and drive myself.")

3:00–8:00 P.M.: workout ("I usually have a
piece of fruit during workout.")

8:20–9:00: drive home ("I drive myself.")

9:00–10:30 or 11:00: dinner, homework,
shower, etc.

Elise explained further, "Monday, Tuesday,
and Wednesday, I follow this schedule. Thurs-
day, we don't have morning practice, just afternoon, so I just go to school at eight-thirty.
Friday, we don't have afternoon practice, just
morning. And Saturday, we go seven to noon,
and Sunday is completely off.

"Kelli really believes in public school," Elise
added. "So do my parents and I, so I have a lot
of support there. I get a lot of homework done
during the school day, in class or at lunch. And
the rest I finish at night."

It's important to Elise to have a well-
balanced life and that means keeping her rela-
tionships going with non-gymnastic friends. "I
have a great group of school friends, so when
I'm not at the gym, I am usually with them,"
Elise elaborated.

Some people have said that young athletes like Elise, Kristen, and Vanessa are missing out on a "normal" life. Very few of these girls have any regrets about the life they lead, however.

"Yes, I've missed out on some stuff," Elise admits, "but compared to all I have gained through the sacrifices I have made, I wouldn't give it up for the world. I still get to be a high school kid and go to homecomings and proms and football games. I just have a whole other special life in the gym. It is so worth it, and it is true, we all have gotten to travel worldwide, and have already had so many lifetime experiences. So as I see it, we have the better hand."

Vanessa Atler admits that she, too, has made sacrifices for the sport she loves and has forgone the usual teenager's social life. "No parties," Vanessa said. "All my friends are in the gym. They're the only ones who understand." But she has no regrets. "Gymnastics has given me so much and taught me so much about myself," she said several years ago. "I know a lot more than most girls my age."

Some gymnasts have had to move several times in their young lives. Morgan White is one of them, but she doesn't feel she's made a big sacrifice. She loves what she does and feels that she's been blessed with opportunities to travel and compete. She admits that a gymnast's life can often be tough, especially juggling school studies and an intense training program, but says she wouldn't have done it if she hadn't been having fun. Morgan also believes she has gotten some very important values out of gymnastics, including hard work, confidence, and belief in herself.

Kristen Maloney agrees. "As I got better, I realized there are so many things I could get out of gymnastics. [Without it,] I don't think I would have the discipline I do. Also the traveling. If I were not in gymnastics, I would never have gotten the opportunity to see all the places that I have. Then of course, there is always the Olympics."

Next Stop:
Sydney 2000

He's Back," the headline read in *USA Gymnastics* magazine. The "he" in question, as the entire gymnastics community knew, was Bela Karolyi, and the big news as the 2000 gymnastics season opened was that he was coming out of retirement to serve as national team coordinator for the women's gymnastics team.

Karolyi, who had guided the careers of champions Nadia Comaneci, Mary Lou Retton, Kerri Strug, Kim Zmeskal, and Dominique Moceanu, retired in 1996 following the Atlanta Games. Then, in late 1999, Karolyi was asked by USA Gymnastics to help formulate the team's training program and oversee the preparation of the 2000 women's Olympic team.

While not officially coaching, Bela and his wife, Martha, would work closely with prospective team members and their coaches, and play a major role in choosing the final team.

Karolyi's experience, knowledge, and ability to motivate and inspire gymnasts were seen as invaluable to a team that was packed with talent but had not yet lived up to its potential. If anyone could bring out the best in the American team, it would be Bela Karolyi.

As the year 2000 began, the final countdown to Sydney started in earnest. The next eight months would determine just who would head for Australia and who would stay home. And it quickly became apparent from Karolyi's comments that no one was guaranteed a spot on the women's Olympic team. They would all have to earn it, he said. "The goal is Sydney," he declared. "No one's position is carved in stone."

A series of training camps in Houston, Texas, was scheduled to begin in January 2000, and twenty-eight of the top women gymnasts would be invited to the first one. Among those hoping to make a comeback were three Magnificent Seven veterans: Dominique Moceanu, Amy Chow, and Jaycie Phelps. Only about half of the gymnasts would be invited back to the second session in March. Karolyi explained that being cut from the camp didn't put a gymnast out of the running. Any gymnast who showed great improvement in the 2000 season would have a chance to make the team.

The gymnasts who were invited back for the March session included 1999 Worlds team members Vanessa Atler, Kristen Maloney, Jeanette Antolin, Jamie Dantzscher, Alyssa Beckerman, Elise Ray, Jennie Thompson, and Morgan White. Former Magnificent Seven member Amy Chow also made the cut. Veteran national team members Erinn Dooley and Marie Fjordholm were also on the list, along with several young hopefuls who had placed in the top twenty at the 1999 Nationals including Annabeth Eberle, age sixteen, of Reno, Nevada, who had placed fifteenth; Dana Pierce, age sixteen, of Lebanon, Indiana (twentieth place); and Tasha Schwikert, age fifteen, of Las Vegas, Nevada (ninth place). Sierra Sapunar, an eighteen-year-old from Sebastopol, California, was also invited back, based on her all-around gold medal at the 1999 U.S. Classic meet.

Missing from the list was Dominique Moceanu. The 1995 national champion and 1996 Olympian had been plagued by injuries and personal problems since 1998. She had also gone through a growth spurt, adding seven inches and 15 pounds to her once tiny frame. In a sport where even a few extra inches can throw off an athlete's performance, those kinds of changes require major and often difficult adjustments to a gymnast's style. Dominique had not been able to train regularly, much less compete, for most of 1999, and she wasn't actually a national team member as 2000 began, but she had begun to work with coach Mary Lee Tracy at the Cincinnati Gymnastics Academy. "She still has a decent chance of making the team if she is able to get back into shape physically," explained USA Gymnastics spokesperson Courtney Caress. "If anyone can get her back, Mary Lee is the one to do it."

By mid-March, Dominique had made sufficient progress to win an invitation to one of Bela Karolyi's training camps in March. The former national champion showed that her talent had not faded, and she was invited back to another training session in May. So was 1997 Worlds team member Lindsay Wing.

Magnificent Seven member Amy Chow was also invited to the second camp. Amy, the first Asian-American to make a U.S. Olympics gymnastics team, had won the silver medal on uneven bars in Atlanta and had played an important role in the U.S. team's gold medal victory. She was only the sixth American woman in gymnastics history to win a medal in an individual event. In 1999, Amy was hampered by an ankle injury, but by early 2000, she felt ready to compete again, with an eye on the Sydney team. She attended one of Bela Karolyi's training camps and impressed onlookers with her performances. "At the training camp, she was one of the best performers," Karolyi commented. "I was very surprised. She's definitely ready for big-time competition again."

Amy certainly came to the training camp with impressive credentials beyond her Olympic medals. She's been on the national team since 1990, and is a two-time Worlds team member. A versatile performer who likes to create original moves all her own, Amy has had two uneven bars moves, the Chow One and Chow Two, named after her. She's an accomplished gymnast with great skills, and she has won gold medals on all four apparatuses during her career. In addition to being a superior gymnast, Amy is also a gifted pianist.

Amy began gymnastics at age three in her hometown of San Jose, California. She originally wanted to be a ballerina, but when her mother tried to enroll her in a dancing class, she was told that Amy was too young. So Amy was signed up for a tumbling class at a local gym instead. Gymnastics lessons followed, and it was not long before Amy began rising up the junior ranks. By 1993 she was competing as a senior. The next year she traveled to Dortmund, Germany, with the World Championships team that brought home a silver medal. At the 1995 Pan Am Games, she won the vault and helped the U.S. women capture the gold. After tying Shannon Miller in the all-around at the Reese's International Gymnastics Cup in 1997, she began attending Stanford University with the goal of becoming a pediatrician. In the spring of 1999, however, she announced that she would take a year off to train for the Olympics.

Amy returned to her original training routine, putting in as many as thirty hours a week. She plans to enter several major meets in 2000, and while she has an uphill battle to make the team, she also has the skills and experience to face that challenge. If proof was needed to back up that claim, she produced it in mid-March. At the Bluewater International meet in Sarnia, Canada, Amy topped an international field of women gymnasts to decisively take the all-around competition gold medal.

If the competition for the 2000 Olympic team wasn't intense enough, the race heated up significantly in February with more big news: Shannon Miller, too, was about to attempt a comeback. Earlier, at the Dynamo Classic in Oklahoma City, Shannon had given a three-event exhibition performance that showed she had lost none of her gifts. Shannon, a graduate of the Dynamo club, offered three superb sets on bars, beam and vault, all featuring moves that were surprisingly difficult for someone who had not been competing regularly since 1998.

At first, Shannon claimed she was only back in the gym to train for a post-Olympic exhibition tour. Convinced her skills were still sharp, however, she declared that she intended to try for a spot on a third Olympic team. As a result, she was invited to the national team training camp in Houston, Texas, so that Bela Karolyi and the national staff could evaluate her current skills. "I'm very excited to see her and give her any help to regain her readiness," Karolyi said.

Shannon, recently married and nearly twenty-three, knew she had her work cut out for her. As she told NBCOlympics.com, "Trying for a third Olympics with only eight months of training," she admitted, "that's a huge challenge. I've always told myself not to limit what

I can do, so I'm going to try it. If it works out, fantastic, and if it doesn't work out, then I don't regret it because I tried." Even if she didn't make it, Shannon would still be considered one of the greatest gymnasts of all time.

Meanwhile, the 2000 season began the way the 1999 season had ended—with some great performances from Elise Ray, 1998 bars champ and 1999 floor exercise gold medalist. Building on the momentum she generated at the 1999 Nationals and Worlds, she showed why Vanessa Atler called her the national team's real hero, as she gave a spectacular performance at January's Aussie Haircare Gymnastics Invitationals. That event—one of three that would make up the important 2000 Visa American Cup competition—drew top-ranked gymnasts from China, Romania, and four other countries. Elise Ray edged out Australia's Allana Slater to win the all-around. Then she dominated the women's Event Finals, taking the gold in vault, uneven bars, and floor exercise. Tasha Schwikert, a last-minute entry in the competition, gave the American team another reason to cheer, with her third-place finish in the all-around.

Tasha had become a member of the national team in 1997 after finishing third in the all-around and second in vault at 1996's

Junior Olympic Championships. In 1999 she gave an impressive performance at the U.S. Classic, winning a silver medal in all-around. She was also a member of the gold medal team at the 1999 China Dual meet. While she failed to earn a medal at the 1999 U.S. Championships, she finished in the top ten in the all-around, the top five in bars, and just missed the bronze medal on vault. In February, Tasha won the American Classic, where she finished nearly a full point ahead of her closest competitor, Monique Chang. With her athleticism and youthful energy, Tasha is clearly a gymnast on the way up. Previously considered a fill-in for injured members of the national team, Tasha suddenly appeared to be a prospective Olympic hopeful.

Morgan White continued her upward progress in 2000 when she competed at the RCA Challenge meet in Las Vegas in January, another qualifying meet for the Visa American Cup. Her marks—8.612 on vault, 9.5 on bars, 9.4 on beam, and 9.025 on floor—put her in fourth place overall, and as the top American finisher, she, along with Elise Ray, would qualify for the finals of the American Cup. Typically, she said she was a little disappointed with her overall performance but was thrilled to have made it to the American Cup finals.

In February, Elise Ray announced she would not compete at the finals in the Visa American Cup because of a stress fracture in her right foot. Elise wasn't happy about missing the meet, but she was glad the injury had come early in the season. "I was really looking forward to [the meet], so I'm very disappointed about it," Elise said. "If it had to happen at all, I'd rather have it happen early in the season, so I can be healthy later." Elise resumed her training in early March, but Tasha Schwikert took her place in the Visa Cup finals in Orlando, Florida.

Morgan White was the American team's best hope in the finals, but at the end of the first rotation, she was in sixth place. In the finals, however, she gave an inspired floor exercise performance that earned loud cheers from the audience and a 9.65, the highest score of the competition. The score boosted her into second place, right behind Russian star Elena Produnova. (Tasha Schwikert finished fourth.) Morgan had been quite anxious, but her solid score put those jitters behind her and gave her plenty of reasons to be optimistic about the new season.

"I've never been so nervous in my entire life!" a beaming Morgan exclaimed at the end of the meet. "The fact that I overcame my nerves and was able to hit all my events just makes me so happy. I know now I can go into any meet and overcome them. It felt so great and the audience was really into it. It pumped me up. It felt so wonderful and it's really exciting."

Jennie Thompson, defending American Cup champion, spent the end of 1999 recuperating from ankle surgery, so she decided against participating in the 2000 American Cup competition. She was disappointed that she would not defend her title, but she and coach Mary Lee Tracy recognized that their main goal was to win an Olympic berth. Any re-injury to the ankle would seriously jeopardize Jennie's chances, so they made plans to start her 2000 season at the Senior Pacific Alliance Championships in April. "Right now we just don't want any more setbacks," Tracy cautioned. Another of Tracy's gymnasts, Alyssa Beckerman, sat out the first part of the 2000 season. However, Alyssa returned to competition in late April and led an American team to a first-place finish at the Spieth-Sogipa Cup meet in Brazil. Alyssa also won the all-around gold medal. The Americans swept the all-around, as Tasha Schwikert and Lindsay Wing won silver and bronze medals in the event.

At the Senior Pacific Alliance Championships,

the American women's team had many reasons to celebrate. First, Elsie Ray, who had
recovered from the fracture in her foot, captured the all-around gold medal and first place
in floor exercise. Morgan White finished third
in the all-around and won a silver on the floor
exercise. Amy Chow placed an encouraging
fifth place in the all-around as the U.S. women
took the team gold, topping a six-team international field.

Sierra Sapunar, another member of Tracy's
Cincinnati Gymnastics Academy, has also been
mentioned as a possible candidate for the
Olympic team. Sierra, who hails from
Sebastopol, California, but now lives in Ohio,
was sidelined for most of 1999 with an elbow
injury, but her previous record showed
tremendous potential. At the 1997 Junior U.S.
Championships, she had won a gold in floor
exercise and a silver in the all-around. The
next year, as a senior, she won several medals
in both national and international meets. By
early 1999, Sierra seemed poised to rise even
higher. At the American Classic, she finished
third in the all-around and tied Elise Ray for
the gold on uneven bars. She followed that
with a gold medal in the all-around at the U.S.
Classic. But at a training session in August
1999 she had a freak accident and fell off the

bars, chipping a bone in her elbow. Sierra's season, which had begun with such promise, was suddenly over. But in early 2000, Sierra's coach, Mary Lee Tracy, said that Sierra would soon be ready to pick up where she had left off. "Her doctor just worked miracles," the veteran coach declared. "Sierra is awesome right now."

No matter who eventually made the final cut, Bela Karolyi, like the gymnasts with whom he was working, knew very well that expectations would remain high for the 2000 Olympic team. After all, thanks to the Magnificent Seven, the 2000 team entered the Olympics as defending champions. As everyone knows, when you're the champion, every other team is all the more eager to knock you off the podium.

Karolyi himself was asked by NBCOlympics.com to compare his current Olympic candidates to the Magnificent Seven. "The 1996 team had more experience on the international floor," he explained. "They already had World Championships behind them; three of them— Kerri Strug, Shannon [Miller], and Dominique Dawes—were previous Olympians. That was a plus. We still have talented people who can form a united and strong team. Maybe we will not have the experience of those girls, but I know we could have the desire, the ambition, the strong, aggressive manner of competing that was characteristic of the American team all the way up to the 1996 Olympic Games. I'm really looking forward to seeing the progress of the team."

So was the entire American gymnastics community. Much, of course, would depend on the results at the 2000 U.S. Gymnastics Championships in July and the Olympic trials scheduled for August in Boston. From those competitions, the final six women Olympians would be chosen. No matter what happened, the Sydney Games in September would be thrilling. For the women hoping to make the trip, it would be impossible not to think about it. As they all knew, and as the Magnificent Seven had proved, anything is possible.

"Thinking about the Olympics gets me a little excited and a little nervous at the same time," Kristen Maloney says. The only thing that can be expected with certainty is the unexpected. Or as Kristen puts it, "You never know what's going to happen."

Gymnastics Events and Scoring

Reporters have described women gymnasts as "diminutive," "petite," and even "pixieish," but when you see them in action, you can't miss their physical prowess and amazing abilities. Gymnastics requires strength, agility, concentration, and split-second timing. It combines a dancer's skills and grace with an acrobat's skills, daring, and courage. This sport demands power and elegance and, perhaps most important, precision. A single slip, distraction, missed move, or fall can spell the difference between triumph and tears.

Women's gymnastics competitions comprise four apparatuses, or events: vault, uneven bars, balance beam, and floor exercise. In most inter-

national competitions, women compete both
as a team and as individuals. In team competition, all the scores by the team members on all
four apparatuses are totaled to come up with a
team score. There is usually also an all-around
competition in which gymnasts compete as
individuals on all four apparatuses, trying to
get the highest combined score. In Event
Finals, individuals compete for themselves on
each apparatus, trying to become the vault,
bars, beam, or floor exercise champion. Usually a gymnast must qualify in earlier rounds
to compete in the Event Finals.

The vault event consists of a runway with a
maximum length of 25 meters (82 feet), a
springboard, and a vaulting horse that is 120
centimeters (approximately 4 feet) tall, 35 cm.
(13.7 inches) wide, and 160 cm. (5.2 feet) long.
Gymnasts sprint down the runway, then, with
explosive power, take off from a springboard.
Using their hands to vault off the horse, they
fly into the air, raising their feet up over their
heads. Once airborne, they perform twisting
flips and other moves before making their dismount or landing. Some gymnasts even do a
move called a round-off, where the gymnast
runs forward, turns her body as she does a
handstand, and flips backward onto the horse.
Proper body, shoulder, and hand position are

critical, as are height and distance traveled in the air. A gymnast must then "stick" her landing, which means she must take no extra steps. Falling on a dismount results in a lower score.

Strength, speed, timing, and fearlessness are all required to be successful on the uneven bars, perhaps the most spectacular of the four events. Gymnasts swing with great speed, moving between the low and high bar, using different grips, releases, and changes in direction. While on the bars, gymnasts do saltos (somersaults or flips), or pirouettes in which they turn in a full circle while doing a handstand on the bar. The routines must flow together smoothly with no extra swings or supports. The low bar is approximately 148 cm. (4.85 feet) off the floor while the high bar is approximately 228 cm. (7.5 feet) high. The bars are 150 cm. (4.9 feet) apart. The action is nonstop, and judges base scores on the degree of difficulty of the routine, on whether the gymnast has completed the elements of each move properly and smoothly, and on the dismount. Even things as seemingly small as a gymnast's leg position and how she points her toes while doing her moves can affect her score.

Imagine doing somersaults, front and back handsprings, flips, splits, and ballet-like leaps on a board 4 inches wide and 4 feet above the floor. That's what's required on the balance beam. The wooden beam is 500 cm. (16.4 feet) long and stands 120 cm. (3.9 feet) high. It is equipped with small springs that give the gymnast extra bounce. A gymnast must combine a delicate balancing act with flips, turns, leaps off the beam, handsprings, and other daring moves, ending with a precise high-flying twisting dismount. To many, this is the most difficult event, since it requires a gymnast to land very precisely every single time. With the beam 4 inches wide, there is little room for error.

Some gymnasts use a springboard to make impressive leaps onto the beam, while others simply lift themselves gracefully onto the beam. Scores are based on how smooth, well connected, and steady the gymnast makes each move and the routine as a whole. Points are also added or deducted based on poise and artistic qualities. Ambitious moves such as double back somersaults earn higher scores, while points are taken away for falls (half a point alone), shakiness, and extra steps on a dismount.

Floor exercise is perhaps the most popular and artistic event in women's gymnastics. It combines dance-like moves, like pirouettes and splits, with tumbling and acrobatic maneuvers such as triple twists, in which the gymnast not only flips over in the air but spins her body around three times as she does so. The routines last from seventy to ninety seconds and are done to music selected by each gymnast. The gymnasts do their routines on a 40-by-40-foot mat that sits on top of a layer of plywood and carpet supported by springs. The gymnast must use all the available space on the mat, but if she steps off it she will be penalized.

Gymnasts are graded on the difficulty of their moves and also on their presentation. Each segment must flow smoothly into the next. In addition to doing amazing acrobatic moves, gymnasts must be graceful, elegant, and expressive. Even hand movements are scrutinized by the judges.

Scoring in gymnastics is very complicated and the sport's Code of Points, which sets up scoring rules for international competition, changes after each Olympics. A new set of scoring criteria became effective in January 1997. Major changes were made in how final scores were tallied, in how many judges should preside, and in the awarding of bonus points. Adjustments were also made in difficulty levels in several events, especially vault, where many start values (a point value based on difficulty) were lowered. Skills in other events were also adjusted, making it harder than ever for a gymnast to score a perfect 10.

In each routine except vault, a gymnast begins with less than a perfect ten. Women gymnasts begin with a 9.00 score; men's scores begin at 8.60. Judges can award bonus points, 1.0 for women and 1.40 for men, based on how well the gymnasts execute their moves and how difficult the moves are. Each routine's elements have a start value, and points can be added depending on how well the moves are executed and presented. Moves are also graded by letters, with A for the easier moves and E for hardest. Judges also deduct points for flaws, poor presentation, and poor landings. Vault, unlike the other three events, starts out with an assigned value up to 10.0. A perfect vault will get the full score, while the gymnast will lose points for flaws or poor landings.

"It's actually more difficult to score a perfect ten on vault since the vaults valued at 10 are now very difficult and not many gymnasts perform 10.0-valued vaults," explains Connie Maloney of USA Gymnastics. "It's also difficult on the other three events because in those events that start at a 9.0, a gymnast has to include either many more D's and E's, or many higher-valued combinations to earn the 1.00 in bonus points." Vault is also challenging because a gymnast must do two vaults, not one. The scores are then averaged together.

Connie explains further: "Basically for uneven bars, balance beam, and floor exercise, if the gymnast fulfills all the difficulty requirements [1A, 2B's, 2C's, 1D] and has met all special requirements of the event [there are seven for each event, worth 0.20 each], the highest score she can achieve is 9.00. She earns the bonus by performing additional difficulties [D's are worth 0.10 bonus; E's are worth 0.2 bonus] or performing skills that have high difficulty value."

Another kind of gymnastics will be featured at the Sydney Games. We've been discussing artistic gymnastics. There is also rhythmic gymnastics, in which performers use ribbons, balls, clubs, hoops, and ropes to create a graceful and flowing dance-like routine on a 42.5-by-42.5-foot carpet. Rhythmic gymnastics requires not only agility, endurance, and flexibility but also strength and power. While not as popular or as well known as artistic gymnastics, rhythmic gymnastics is quite beautiful to watch.

Glossary

aerial: a move in which a gymnast turns over in midair, without touching the apparatus with her hands.

amplitude: the height a gymnast achieves in an airborne portion of the routine. This can be an important element in scoring.

apparatus: a piece of equipment used in gymnastics—for example, the uneven bars, the vaulting horse, the pommel horse, the still rings, or the balance beam.

arch position: a position in which the body is curved backward.

dismount: a move done when the gymnast leaves the apparatus at the end of a routine. Dismounts are often done with high-flying twists or saltos.

execution: a gymnast's performance of her routine. Form, body position, style, and technique are all part of the execution.

flic-flic, or flip-flop: a back handspring in which the gymnast flips backward off one or both feet, lands on her hands, then swings her feet over as she pushes off with her arms, eventually landing back on her feet. This move is often done on beam.

handspring: a move in which the gymnast springs off her hands to propel herself into the air. A handspring can be done forward or backward.

layout: a body position in which the gymnast keeps her body straight or slightly arched.

pike: a position or move in which the gymnast keeps her body bent forward more than 90 degrees at the hips while her legs remain straight.

pirouette: a move in which the gymnast changes direction in a full 360-degree circle as she stands on one leg or does a handstand. Pirouettes are often done in floor exercise and uneven bars.

round-off: a turning, cartwheel-like move in which a gymnast pushes off one leg, then swings her legs upward quickly, turning her body 90 degrees as she does so. When the gymnast brings her feet down to the mat, she will be facing in the direction opposite to the one she started in.

salto: a somersault or flip in which the gymnast brings her feet over her head while she rotates her body around the axis of her waist.

stick: to nail a landing without taking a step to regain one's balance. It's as if the gymnast's feet "stick" to the mat upon landing.

tuck: a move in which the gymnast is bent at the waist with her knees pulled up toward her chest.

twist: a movement in which a gymnast spins or rotates her body along the axis of the spine.

Yurchenko: a vault in which the gymnast does a round-off onto the springboard, then does a back handspring onto the horse. The move is then completed with a layout, a full twist, a one-and-a-half twist, or a double twist.

Gymnastics
Web Sites

If you're interested in learning more about gymnastics or your favorite gymnast, these Web sites offer personal home pages for the Worlds team members, for gymnastics organizations such as USA Gymnastics, and for magazines such as *International Gymnast*. You can also follow gymnastics competitions at the Sydney Olympic Games at nbcolympics.com. The sites listed below offer many other avenues to explore:

USA GYMNASTICS
http://www.usa-gymnastics.org

ELISE RAY
http://www.eliseray.net

VANESSA ATLER
http://www.atler.com/

KRISTEN MALONEY
http://www.parkettes.com/kristen

JENNIE THOMPSON
http://www.angelfire.com/nj/Gymnast339/index.html

JAMIE DANTZSCHER
http://www.gymn.com/jamied/

JEANETTE ANTOLIN
http://www.angelfire.com/ca/jantolin/

ALYSSA BECKERMAN
http://www.alyssabeckerman.net/

MORGAN WHITE
http://www.geocities.com/Colosseum/Pressbox/4636/

NBC OLYMPICS COVERAGE
http://www.nbcolympics.com/

INTERNATIONAL GYMNAST MAGAZINE
http://www.intlgymnast.com/

INTERNATIONAL GYMNASTICS FEDERATION
http://www.gymnastics.worldsport.com

U.S. OLYMPIC COMMITTEE
http://www.olympic-usa.org

About the Author

CHIP LOVITT is the author of more than three dozen children's books, including *Inventions No One Mentions; The Great Rock 'n' Roll Photo Quiz Book; The Ultimate Disney Joke Book;* and a variety of sports books, including biographies of Michael Jordan, Charles Barkley, Magic Johnson, and Nancy Kerrigan. He lives in New Milford, Connecticut, with his son, Keith.

WNBA

STARS OF WOMEN'S BASKETBALL

Take to the courts with league MVP Cynthia Cooper. Go eye to eye with unblinking Sheryl Swoopes. Pound the boards with superstar and supermodel Lisa Leslie. And see what's *really* happening in the red-hot game of women's basketball! Here's everything you need to know about the teams—and the players—that are putting the bad-boy superstars of the NBA in their place. Packed with photos, stats, profiles, interviews, team spotlights, and Q&As, this slam-dunking book tells the amazing stories behind these phenomenal players.

INSIDE STORIES YOU WON'T SEE ANYWHERE ELSE!

by James Ponti

Now available!

An Archway Paperback
Published by Pocket Books

2114